FROM THE
INSIDE OUT

I. B. Nobody

Fulton Books, Inc.
Meadville, PA

First originally published by Fulton Books 2017

ISBN 978-1-63338-316-6 (Paperback)
ISBN 978-1-63338-317-3 (Digital)

Printed in the United States of America

Not another golf book . . .

More than fifty years ago, this author began assembling observations and notes of this great game in what I've come to call *From the Inside Out*. The impetus for this book was twofold: one, a library filled with golf books that my daughter couldn't care less about; two, and most importantly, presenting a concept to golfdom as to how to k.i.s.s.—keep it simple, stupid.

This is an instructional manual covering the fundamentals of the golf swing, the short game, routine development, putting, the mental game, creating a feeling storehouse, concentration and temperment. Also, a ***historical*** look at the greats and not so greats of the game - circa 1920, to the Tiger Woods era. Included are the individuals who influenced my development as a golfer, a caddie's view from inside the ropes, and a look at the world of golf from the inside out. This book also contains quotes and references from over 40 different World of Golf Hall of Fame members. From Greg Norman you'll learn the true meaning of the game of golf. Like Boxing? Heavyweight champions Joe Louis and Muhammed Ali are referenced. If you're a baseball fan: Babe Ruth, George Wright, Sam Byrd, Joe D, Ted Williams, Jackie Robinson, Yogi Berra & Mickey Mantle all made the final edits.

Any player—no matter the skill level—hitting a golf ball does so in three steps:
*   Set up to the ball
*   Swing at the ball
*   Create an impact

This sets up this framework . . .

I.   Setup
II.   Swing
III. Impact

Within those roman numerals are eight fundamentals, obtained from Ben Hogan's book, *Ben Hogan's Five Lessons: The Modern Fundamentals of Golf.* The book, which began as a series of five articles that first appeared in the magazine *Sports Illustrated* on March 11, 1957, evolved into a book that was published in the latter part of 1957. You are encouraged to read or reread *Five Lessons* as Hogan's swing theory will become that much clearer. Each of the aforementioned eight fundamentals are supported by quotes from some of the masters—Bobby Jones, Gene Sarazen, Walter Hagen, Byron Nelson, Sam Snead, Ben Hogan (Snead, Hogan, and Nelson were all born within seven months of one another in 1912. Collectively, they won almost 200 PGA tour events!). Countless players were inspired by these greats—Arnold Palmer, Jack Nicklaus, Gary Player, Billy Casper, Lee Trevino, Tom Watson; Northern California products: Tony Lema, Ken Venturi, Bob Rosburg, John Brodie, George Archer, Bob Boldt, Dick Lotz, John Lotz, Johnie Miller, Ross Randle, Roger Maltbie, Forrest Fezler, John Abendroth, Shivas Irons, and many, many other great players. Let's not forget two who competed with Sarazen, Hagen, et al: Olin Dutra and Lawson Little, Jr. *From the Inside Out* also includes quotes from one of golf's finest instructor, Percy Boomer.

For those that learn visually, the pictures and diagrams alone will give you a greater understanding of the golf swing.

In my quest to become a great player, many a hour was spent on the practice tee as a thorough, diligent student. While seeking instruction, my criteria was that the instructor, at some point in his life, had to have shot 6 under par. While taking those golf lessons from past champions and excellent instructors, meticulous notes were kept (those notes are detailed in the chapter "Golf Lessons from the 6 Under Par Club"). As a mechanic, in the application of what had been taught, balls were pounded until the blisters bled. Turning all that instruction into muscle memory required many hours of practice and many "good walks spoiled" around the links.

As a player? Flashes of brilliance, playing to a single-digit index from 1968 to now . . . hovering around or below scratch when playing four to five times per week. Highlights included qualifying for the 1971 US Public Links Championship, 1975 US Amateur Championship, and advancing into the regional qualifying tournament for the 1976 US Open. Bobby Jones would say I played in a major championship. In the whole scheme of things, I'm really a nobody in the game of golf. Hence, the pseudonym I. B. Nobody.

If you are a beginner, it's best to start with Getting Started on page 186. Focus heavily on the grip section of the book, especially its nuances. If you're a right-hander, start with a strong left-hand grip (meaning that you can see two knuckles of your left hand when looking down at your grip) and work your way to a weaker grip as you progress. Just the opposite if you're a left-handed golfer—strong right-hand grip.

The best part of purchasing this book? Eighty eight percent of the proceeds from the sale of this book will be evenly evenly distributed to The First Tee, the Ben Hogan Foundation, the Jim Langley Scholarship Fund and the University of Kansas's golf program in memory of Ross Randle. The other twelve percent will go to the publisher, lawyers, and what remains will go to St. Jude's, green fees and gratuties for those in the golf shops. A special note of thanks to the Ben Hogan Foundation for permission to use the photos/illustrations contained in this book. They are invaluable.

On a personal note, this book offers an opportunity to step back into time and learn what the masters of the game thought or more importantly, what they felt. These nuggets of information have emanated from the masters of the game & most excellent players. . .they are still applicable today. Not only are the proceeds targeted to the youth of America, it is worth the price of admission as it will provide a real glimpse of the crown prince of golf - Walter Hagen.

It has been said golf is 20 percent mechanics and technique, the other 80 percent is philosophy, humor, tragedy, romance, melodrama, companionship, camaraderie, cussedness, and concentration. Intended to be shared with golfdom, hopefully, you will consider it a tangible contribution to the great game. As Jimmy Demaret (winner of the 1940, 1947 & 1951 Masters) once said, "Golf and sex are the only things you can enjoy without being good at them." Enjoy!

The main idea in golf, as in life, I suppose, is to
learn to accept what cannot be altered, and to keep
on doing one's own reasoned and resolute best
whether the prospects be bleak or rosy.

—Bobby Jones

There is a school of Oriental philosophy, I am told,
which holds that the aim of life should be the perfection
of personality or character and the sufferings, joys,
and achievements mean nothing except as the influence
of the development of this personality or character.

—Bobby Jones

In the end Palmer's major championship disappointments
shaped him more than his triumphs. "Losing," he said,
"you just got to learn from losing."

I played 365 rounds of golf last year. Thank God for
whoever invented golf. I'd been dead without it.

—Babe Ruth

Foreword

Of the many instructional books available, it is a pleasure to have yours; in its common-sense approach with tips from the greats to augment the simple swing principles and drawing from your experiences and anecdotes, I. B. Nobody touches us with the lessons learned of golf and life.

I only wish I had known Mr. Bateman. but knowing him through you ensures his legacy, and for that, our world is a little better place.

For all of us searching for the perfect lesson we need search no further. I. B. Nobody has it all.

Jim Langley
PGA Golf Professional
Cypress Point Club
September 26, 2006

Contents

Golf Circa 1920

Babe Ruth

The 1920's was the decade of new consumption. World War I had primed American industry for the mass production of consumer goods. The Highway Act of 1921 spurred growth in interstate trucking, and facilitated the delivery of those goods. The electrification of factories and households stimulated a national spending spree. The big names of the times were, aviator Charles Lindberg; gangster Al Capone; boxer Jack Dempsey; scientist Albert Einstein; singer Al Jolson; motion picture star Charlie Chaplin and musician Duke Ellington. Bobby Jones was a celebrity to golf fans but there weren't many of them. In contrast, Babe Ruth was the most famous athlete in the world. He reached a level of fame that redefined fame. He restored America's faith in baseball after the 1919 Black Sox scandal, and played a huge role in making golf a spectator sport in America. Ruth made the game look like fun, and his passion for golf motivated millions of Americans, who never played the rich man's sport, to pick up a club. Babe Ruth was once America's most famous golfer.

Ruth was 20 when he first took up the game – in fact, received the news that he was being traded from the Red Sox to the Yankees while on the golf course. Alex Morrison, at the time golf guru to the stars – he pioneered swing sequence photos by hanging a lantern from a club swung in a dark room – taught the Babe to play. Ruth could arguably be the man who pioneered celebrity golf, playing in numerous matches with the most famous golfers & celebrities of the times. No question, he was the first famous left handed golfer and played a MAJOR role in popularizing the game in America. "A golfer could drain a flask of whiskey while playing and eat a hot dog (or three) between holes...what a game!" Why he's not in the World Golf

Hall of Fame is anybody's guess. As Babe's daughter, Dorothy, once said, "Baseball broke his heart but golf kept him going."

Alex J. Morrison

Born in California in 1896, at age 12 he began caddying at The Los Angeles Country Club. By 1920 he had become a noted teacher and exhibition golfer traveling the vaudeville circuit. Alex Morrison had a thread that ran through the three best golfers of all time. Each of the three had signIficant teachers/mentors with definite ideas on what was important. Bobby Jones; East Lake Country Club's head pro, Stewart Maiden, who instructed young Bobby, subscribed to much of what Morrison taught. Ben Hogan; most significantly, learned to weaken his grip from Henry Picard who spent 8 days with Morrison learning his fundamentals. Hogan dedicated his first book, Power Golf to Picard. Jack Nicklaus; Jack Gout, Nicklaus's long time instructor, learned the basics first hand from from Henry Picard. Picard had his greatest success while changing from a Vardon grip to an interlocking grip.

Morrison believed in simplified instruction. "By simply giving their attention to one or two points I suggest they will automatically bring their shoulders, hips & legs into the proper action. These 2 points will help every player no matter what shot he is having difficulty with: standing erect as he can and keep his chin pointed to the back of the ball."

Morrison also believed that there are 3 parts of the body that must be taken care of if there is to be anything like muscular coordination in the swing:

1. Upper section of the spinal column which affords freedom of action to the shoulders, arms, and hand. This source is kept open by the proper pointing of the chin.
2. Lower section of the spinal column which affords freedom of action with the legs and feet. This is kept open by the side motion of the hips.
3. Wrist joints. This source is kept free partly by having the hands on the club at the same angle.

Look after these three main points of freedom and you can always make your swing one continuous motion. The pointing of the chin is the connecting link, in a sense, between the body and the arms and hands.

Morrison also believed that weight shift is essential in a good golf swing, firmly rooted in good footwork, balance, and the proper rolling of the ankles. The left ankle rolling right on the backswing, the right ankle rolling left on the through swing. He stressed that you must picture the swing as a whole - or one continuous motion - not as a series of separate actions. He believed that golf was 90% mental, 8% physical and 2% mechanical.

Golf was an almost exclusively upper-class sport in the 1920s. There were relatively few public courses and private clubs were too expensive for almost anyone but the rich to join. 3 golfers symbolized golf in the 1920s and they were so colorful that millions followed their exploits.

The Big Three: Robert Tyre "Bobby" Jones, who remained an amateur, the other two were professionals, Walter Hagen and Gene Sarazen

Jones was more typical of the nation's golfers. He was from a wealthy Atlanta family and began playing golf at a very young age. He won a children's tournament at age 6 and played in the top amateur tournaments from his early teen years. He also graduated from Georgia Tech University with a degree in mechanical engineering and later received a degree in English from Harvard. He read for the law, was admitted to the Georgia bar and practiced law while playing in the world's best golf tournaments.

Beginning in 1923 at age 21, Jones was the dominant figure in golf for 7 years, winning the U.S. Open 4 times, the British Open 3 times, the U.S. Amateur 5 times, and the British Amateur once. He retired from competitive golf after winning the Grand Slam of the time in 1930. After retiring as a competitive golfer, Jones practiced law, designed golf clubs, and founded both the Augusta National Golf Club and its fabled tournament, the Masters. He continued to host the Masters tournament until his death in 1971.

Hagen was the son of a blacksmith in Rochester, New York, and he learned the rudiments of golf by practicing in a field while herding cows. He caddied at an exclusive country club where the professional taught him the finer points of the game. He also worked as a taxidermist. A great natural athlete, Hagen turned down a try-out with the Philadelphia Phillies at age 21, in order to play in the 1914 U.S. Open, which he won. Hagen won the U.S. Open again in 1919, and the British Open 4 times in the 1920s, as well as 5 PGA championships.

At that time there was a stark difference between amateurs and professionals in golf. At some private clubs, especially in England, professionals were allowed on the golf course, but not in the locker room, because they were not considered "gentlemen." This class distinction was reflective of American society at that time, but Hagen's success and insistence on better treatment of professionals was a large factor in breaking down some of the class barriers in golf. Hagen brought the golf professional out of the shop and into the clubhouse.

Sarazen (born Eugene Saraceni, and the son of a carpenter), from Harrison, New York. Sarazen is one of five players, (along with Ben Hogan, Gary Player, Jack Nicklaus, and Tiger Woods) to win each of the four majors at least once, now known as the Career Grand Slam: U.S. Open (1922, 1932), PGA Championship (1922, 1923, 1933), The Open Championship (1932), and Masters Tournament (1935). Sarazen became more Hagen's rival in the 1930s and was too young to play much against Jones, but Sarazen was a popular player because of his outgoing nature and because he came from such a humble background. He garnered a huge following among "common people", who had previously had no interest in golf. Sarazen played golf into his 80's, was a golf commentator on Shell's Wonderful World of Golf television show, and was a TV broadcaster at important events. He invented the modern sand wedge, and made golf seem like something for more than just the very rich.

At age 71, Sarazen made a hole-in-one at The Open Championship in 1973, at the "Postage Stamp" at Troon in Scotland. In 1992, he was voted the Bob Jones Award, the highest honor given by the United States Golf Association in recognition of distinguished sportsmanship in golf. Sarazen had what is still the longest-running endorsement contract in professional sports – with Wilson Sporting Goods from 1923 until his death, a total of 75 years.

Ben Hogan

Most of the actual swing instructions in this book are based on the teachings in the book *Ben Hogan's Five Lessons*. Why? Jack Nicklaus and Tiger Woods, unlike Hogan, had a teaching pro(s) instructing them on the fundamentals and nuances of the game. Hogan did not have the luxury of using high-speed cameras, 3D motion-analysis, launch monitors, putting apps, force plates, ShotLink data and a myriad of coaches. Even though he wrote his book in 1957, much of what Hogan said, when examined closely, holds true today. So it is no surprise that *Five Lessons* is a focal point of every serious golfer's library. Larry Nelson, winner of 3 major championships - 1981 & 1987 PGA Championships and the 1983 U.S. Open - and inducted into the World Golf Hall of Fame in October of 2006, had this to say, "This book, Ben Hogan's Modern Fundamentals of Golf, taught me the swing. Although I don't swing like Hogan, what I learned from his book helped me to progress more quickly than anyone would have guessed. The lessons could be done one at a time and the illustrations allowed me to work on the fundamentals myself. I would practice one lesson until I had it down, and then go onto the next. I still refer to the book when my swing gets off." Hogan could be called the father of modern instruction—in which the big muscles of the body, rather than hands, as the controlling influences in the swing. Bennie Hogan would become the champion of figuring things out for himself. Bennie Hogan could stay on the practice tee like nobody else. Bennie Hogan's diligence was amazing, because he had no model for it, and because he got no almost no immediate rewards from it.

"No teacher, the story goes, ever gave him a lesson. Everything he managed to learn about the golf swing—which apparently was twice as much as anybody ever had before him—he dug out of the dirt by practicing until his hands bled. When the skin of his palms blistered and cracked open, he soaked his hands in pickle brine to toughen them for the long haul."

Early in his career, Hogan studied almost every movement Walter Hagen made on a golf course, quickly coming to the conclusion that the Haig possessed the finest natural rhythm and playing tempo any champion ever displayed—which he attempted to copy. In a remarkable handwritten, fourteen page letter to a friend in the late 1960s using a "stick figure" he drew to illustrate his point, Hogan explained the grip, and fundamentals of "a sound driver swing" that he claimed to have developed directly from conversations with the aging Hagen. It detailed principles of a proper grip, finger pressure, alignment of shoulders and feet, flex of knees, position of the body and head through the swing, position of the left hand during the backswing, transfer of weight, and a high finish that encouraged the hips and shoulders to full turn into the shot. Hogan advised: "Keep on file and refer to when in doubt. If used correctly, you can belt the ball a country mile," then concluded his remarkable tutorial by offering a detailed if somewhat unorthodox way of verifying the correctness of one's backswing: "At the top of the backswing the groin muscle on the inside of your right leg near your right nut will tighten. This subtle feeling of tightness there tells you that you have made the correct move back from the ball."

"In the 1930's, sitting with Valerie in her father's empty darkened movie theater, an unknown Ben Hogan had studied Movietone footage of Jones, Hagen and Sarazen in their prime to learn proper hip turn technique and balance. During his embryonic days on tour, he'd studied MacDonald Smith's beautiful swing and spoke with "Wild Bill" Mehlhorn about his cerebral analytical approach to the game. Later, he blended elements picked up from Kyle Laffoon, Lefty Stackhouse, and Jack Burke Sr; Paul Runyon's short game wizardry, Picard's unruffled ease, Denny Shute's mastery with a two iron, and Johnny Revolta's pre-shot waggle also played an invaluable role in Ben's self tutorials in the field. It was his driven experimentation to create a swing that wouldn't wilt under pressure."

"Bill Mehlhorn, another top player of the twenties who always seemed to wind up in second place through nobody's fault but his own, was also saying good-bye to pro golf. Like Walter Hagen, Mehlhorn was a fabulous ball-striker who came to golf from baseball, and he had no shortage of intricate theories about the golf swing and what made it either flop or work. Among other things, Mehlhorn believed a free and natural swing was the only way to hit a ball to the target. But even more important, after playing with Harry Vardon in 1921, Mehlhorn worked for thirteen months to replace his natural hook with a consistent left to right motion - a la Vardon - he came to believe was essential for reliable shot making, a controlled fade. One of the no name hopefuls of the new decade who watched Mehlhorn and attempted to copy his powerful sideways swing, before he vanished from the tour for good, was young Ben Hogan. He was a voracious learner who not only took note of Wild Bill's careful playing action, but paid particular attention to the highly analytical manner in which Mehlhorn considered the golf swing. He then broke it down, and attempted to figure it out in minute detail. Hogan later said that Mehlhorn was the first 'theorist' who got him thinking in depth about the physics of the golf swing."

Question from a 1991 ESPN interview with Ken Venturi: "The Ben Hogan work ethic. . .who instilled that in you?" Hogan: "Hennie Bogan"

Hogan often referred unashamedly to the little man on his shoulder he called Hennie Bogan.

Hogan carried his practice balls in his golf bag. He would dump them on the ground, then hit them to the kid he had hired to stand out in a field to act as a target and shag balls. His fantasy companion, Hennie Bogan, would watch. Hennie was an insatiable practicer, and greater golfer than the great Bobby Jones. Hennie told Ben to hit more balls.

"Bennie and Byron would put in hour after hour on the practice tee, something unheard of. The old timers in golf rarely practiced. They'd take a few swings and then go out and play in a tournament."
Jimmy Damaret

"Asked some years later which great player he would select if he needed one shot to win a major tournament, Bobby Jones unhesitatingly replied, "that's not hard for me to answer - Hogan." He thought a moment and added, "He had the intangible assets - the spiritual."

"I was mostly known for the way I hit my driver." Sam Snead said. "But the truth was, beginning in early '49, I begun concentratin' more on my iron play and puttin' than I ever had before. Most folks didn't realize that's what won all them tournaments for me, and why I had the lowest scorin' average in 1950. In some ways I owed that to Ben. He showed what a fella could do if he put his mind to it. If we hadn't been such competitors then, why, we might have become very good friends. But even when he was out of it I always knew he was out there watchin', counting the days until he could get back."

"Watching Hogan was like watching the great teachers of the East." says Michael Murphy. "In India, in Sanskrit, they have a word that applied perfectly to Hogan - diksha.

Literally translated, it means 'initiation' or even 'transmission.' Anyone who ever watched Ben practice or play felt this diksha, a field of extraordinary psychic energy, a powerful presence that explains why top players and ordinary fans alike found him so irresistible - they would just stand for hours without saying a word, almost as if they were in a church. If you ask anyone who did this, who experienced Hogan's diksha, they'll tell you the silence surrounding him at these times was profound, holy. We in America don't produce mystics. But Hogan was close."

"There's no doubt in my mind that Ben Hogan played a key role in transforming professional golf into something different than it had been, a much bigger game with all kinds of new commercial possibilities. Love him or hate him, most of us were frankly in awe of the man for what he'd done - even before we realized the huge debt of gratitude we owed him." Arnold Palmer

"If you ever heard Hogan hit a ball." says Ben Crenshaw flatly, "it was like no other sound in golf."

I. B. Nobody's Philosophies

The great players
*   Adhere to a few time-proven mechanical fundamentals and resist the passing gimmick
*   Maximize their greatest natural physical assets in molding and maintaining a playing method
*   Have the ability, while playing, to define objectives and then concentrate on achieving them to the exclusion of all else
*   Have desire, intensity, focus

With regard to the golf swing (check out the swing photo sequences of the greats),
*   They turn their shoulders 90 degrees on the backswing around a relatively motionless head
*   They have a true pivot—their weight shifts inside the right leg
*   The downswing is initiated by the lower body—having enough lateral motion to get the weight on the left side—and then drag the clubhead into impact
*   Then facing target with their belly button at the finish

Some of the secrets of the game . . .

"You must learn to feel the sensations through your intellect and then forget them intellectually and leave them to your muscular memory or control system." Percy Boomer.

"You must not think or reflect; you must feel what you have to do." Percy Boomer.

"What we use imagination for is to translate theory into feeling." Percy Boomer.

"Imagination is more important than knowledge." Albert Einstein.

Truisms of the game:

"The hands and arms are passive and the shoulders and hips are active." Percy Boomer.

"What do the hands do? The answer is nothing active until after the arms have moved on the downswing to a position just above the level of the hips." Ben Hogan.

"My belief is quite the contrary, being, briefly, that complete relaxation and ease of motion is necessary to the accomplishment of a rhythmic stroke of any length, from the shortest putt to the full drive. One cannot start with the intention of making any stroke with the hands alone, or with the arms alone, or with anything else alone and hope to swing the club easily and with smooth rhythm. The effort to exclude any part or parts of the body from the action, to hold any part motionless, must set up a strain opposing the ease of movement that is so necessary." Bobby Jones.

"The three basic feels of the golf swing—the pivot, the shoulders moving in response to the pivot, and the arms moving in response to the shoulders. These are the three basic movements of a connected and therefore controlled swing, and they must all be built into the framework of your feel of the swing." Percy Boomer.

LEFT BRAIN
Commands
How a math teacher teaches

RIGHT BRAIN
Pictures, feelings, abstracts
How Picasso paints

In order to play respectable golf, one must learn the fundamentals via left brain and transform those *thoughts*—via right brain—into *pictures, feelings*, and on a much higher level, *abstracts*.

The Fundamentals

Within the book, *Five Lessons* by Ben Hogan, are eight fundamentals. These fundamentals framed in this outline are the cornerstone of *From the Inside Out* ideas/concept/teachings about the golf swing.

About the fundamentals:
1. No golfer can make headway in this game without understanding them.
2. The idea is to stick with and work at these fundamentals.
3. Any golfer who is committed to change can improve as long as he works on them.

The first four fundamentals constitute the *Setup* and fundamentals 4 through 8 constitute the *Swing*.

I. Set Up
  * Grip, Arms – Setting up the triangle
  * Lower Body: Stance, Posture, Ball Position
  * Alignment
  * Waggling

II. Swing
  * Takeaway
  * Staying on Plane throughout the Backswing
  * Initiating the Downswing
  * Hitting through in One Cohesive Movement

III. Impact

Once you understand impact you're on your way to becoming a better golfer. After all, the ball's *spinning* every time you strike it

DIRECTION OF BLOW

DIRECTION OF SPIN IMPARTED TO BALL

PROJECTED PATH OF CLUB HEAD

I. Setup

The single most important maneuver in golf is your setup. It consists of the golfer aligning himself properly to the target, then positioning his/her body in such a way the he/she can move freely during the swing while in balance. Setting up properly will help accomplish the goal of creating power with the big muscles and then transferring it to the clubhead. The setup is where your adjustments are made. The best players have an unvarying setup routine that they execute before addressing the ball, and then run through a series of "setup feels" as they address the ball.

"It is essential to standardize the approach to every shot, beginning even before taking the address position." Bobby Jones.

"The difference between the good and the ordinary golfer is that the good one feels his shots through his address." Percy Boomer.

"The only way in which we can repeat correct shots time after time (and this is the greatest of golfing assets) is to be able to repeat the correct feel of how they are produced." Percy Boomer.

"I feel that hitting specific shots—playing the ball to a certain place in a certain way—is 50 percent mental picture, 40 percent setup, and 10 percent swing. That is why setting up takes me so long, why I have to be so deliberate." Jack Nicklaus.

"I never hit a shot, even in practice, without having a very sharp, in-focus picture of it in my head. It's like a color movie. First I 'see' the ball where I want it to finish, nice and white and sitting up high on the bright green grass. Then the scene quickly changes and I see the ball going there; its path, its trajectory, and shape, even its behavior on landing. Then there's a sort of fade out, and the next scene shows me making the kind of swing that will turn the previous images into reality. Only at the end of this short, private, Hollywood spectacular do I select a club and step up to the ball." Jack Nicklaus.

Grip

There are three types of grips employed by golfers today:

Vardon Overlap - popularized by the great British champion, Harry Vardon, this device has the little finger of his right hand in the gap created by the forefinger & middle finger of his left hand, as a result of which the grip came to be know as the Vardon Overlap. One of the most widely used among great players and the one most commoningly taught on the nation's lesson tees. We will use this grip as a basis of instruction.

Interlocking - popularized by the greatest player in the game, Jack Nicklaus, this device has the little finger of his right hand inter-twined with the forefinger of his left hand. Tom Kite, Michelle Wie, Rory McElroy, Jordan Speith, to name but a few, also use the inter-locking grip.

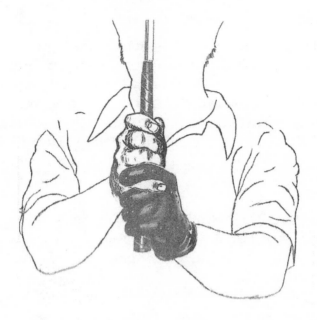

10 Finger or Baseball Grip - Some teachers like to advocate that junior players use the 10-finger grip, with the goal of switching to overlap or interlock later. This is feasible, as kids usually adapt swing and set up changes fairly easily as compared to adults. People with weaker hands and forearms may also benefit from the 10-finger grip. Golfers who use larger arthritic grips may experience that the overlap or interlock is difficult to incorporate with such grips, finding the 10-finger grip offers a greater use of ease. Explained in greater detail on page 181

Whatever grip you choose know that:

A good grip helps shapes your swing correctly and influences the overall tone of the swing – its rhythm and smoothness.

"In a good grip both hands act as one unit. The grip is the heartbeat of the action of the golf swing." Ben Hogan

Left Hand

"With the back of your left hand facing the target (and the club in the general position it would be at address) place the club in the left hand so that (1) the shaft is pressed up under the muscular pad at the inside heel of the palm and (2) the shaft also lies directly across the top joint of the forefinger.

Crook the forefinger around the shaft and you will discover that you can lift the club and maintain a fairly firm grip on it by supporting it just with the muscles of that finger and the muscles of the pad of the palm.

Now just close the left hand—close the finger before you close the thumb—and the club will be just where it should be." Ben Hogan

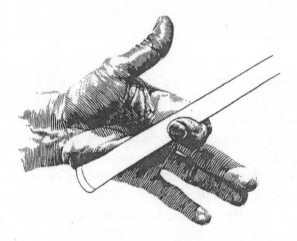

Right Hand

"The right hand grip is almost entirely a finger grip. Encircle the club shaft with your right hand and slide it snugly up next to your left hand, letting your thumb ride comfortably across the top of the handle and making sure the V-shaped crease formed by the thumb and forefinger of this hand also points to your right shoulder. Your right little finger over-laps (or interlocks with) the forefinger of the left hand on the underside of the club handle. In a kind of "pinch," and as a result there will be a slight gap or separatioin between the forefingers and the other fingers. The security and control in the right hand grip comes from the "pinch" and from the marriage of the right little finger of the left forefinger through the overlap or interlock." Sam Snead

"The muscles of the right forefinger and thumb connect with the very powerful set of muscles that run along the outside of the right arm and elbow to the right shoulder. If you work the tips of the thumb and forefinger together and apply any considerable amount of pressure, you automatically activate those muscles of the right arm and shoulder—and those are not the muscles you want to use in the golf swing." Ben Hogan

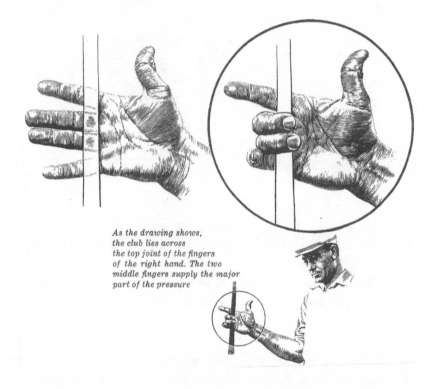

As the drawing shows, the club lies across the top joint of the fingers of the right hand. The two middle fingers supply the major part of the pressure

"A word further about the thumb area of the right hand: school yourself when you are taking your grip so that the thumb extension of the forefinger—press up against each other *tightly*. Keep them pressed together as you begin to affix your grip and maintain this airtight pressure between them when you fold the right hand over the left thumb. In this connection, I like to feel that the knuckle on the back of my right hand above the forefinger is pressing to the left, toward the target. Furthermore, when you fold the right hand over the left thumb—and there is a lot to fold over—the left thumb will fit perfectly in the cup formed in the palm of your folded right hand. They fit together like pieces in a jigsaw puzzle." Ben Hogan

"The pressure points in the grip are the last three fingers of the left hand and the forefinger and thumbs and the little finger of the right hand." Walter Hagen.

"The only way I know of achieving a relaxed grip which will at the same time retain adequate control of the club is to actuate the club and hold it mainly by the three small fingers of the left hand." Bobby Jones.

"Whatever you do, make sure your left hand dominates your right—or vice versa if you're a lefthander—from the time you take hold of the club until you finish the swing. If you hold the club with the same pressure in each hand, your naturally stronger right hand will over power your left hand and take control of the swing, with disastrous results." Byron Nelson.

"I don't ever remember losing the club in my left hand once in my entire life." Byron Nelson.

"In a way, the last two fingers of my left hand are a focal point for my sense of rhythm—a kind of band leaders baton—holding up the drums while the violin finishes." Sam Snead.

"He showed me the classic overlap, or Vardon, grip—the proper grip for a good golf swing—and told me to go hit the golf ball . . . I worked hard to learn the grip Pap showed me. It probably helped that my hands were larger than the average kid's . . . that was pretty much all the swing instruction he gave me for many years. *'Get the right grip, hit the ball hard. Go find the ball, boy, and hit it hard again,'*" Arnold Palmer.

"The standard grip is the overlapping grip or the Vardon grip. Harry Vardon popularized it both in Great Britian and America. In a good grip both hands act as *one unit*. The grip is the heartbeat of the action of the golf swing." Ben Hogan

"I've felt my swing would not fail if I held the club a certain way, that would repeat every time." Dave Eichelberger said. "To me, that's what Hogan's secret was."

Arms - Setting up the Triangle

"Keeping the arms together and pinching the knees together in unison." Walter Hagen.

"Ben Hogan used to practice the swing with his arms bound together by a belt around his forearms. He wasn't trying to stress the differing positions of the left arm and the right arm that ide-ally occupy throughout the swing, but rather to encourage them to work in a balanced and thus harmonious fashion. I think of keeping my elbows together a lot, for the same reason. I also press my knees toward each other when I stand up to the ball, as though I'm slightly knock-kneed—again, in part, to help create a good working relation-ship between opposite sides." Sam Snead.

"The arms work absolutely subjectively to the shoulders, that is why they are controlled. The triangle formed by our arms and a line between the shoulders never loses its shape . . . it should be possible to push a wooden snooker triangle in between the arms and to leave it there without impeding the swing back or through." Percy Boomer.

"Most people think they lift their arms to get them to the top of the backswing. With a modern controlled swing they do not lift them . . . the arms work absolutely subjective to the shoulders, that is why they are controlled." Percy Boomer.

"It is by the management of the arms that championships are won or lost." Percy Boomer.

"Keep your left arm connected against your chest, the same as a baseball batter or forehand down the line in tennis or anything else - the lead arm always stays on the body. It all came from baseball and Babe Ruth, teaching Sam Byrd how to bat. A drill—a handkerchief under the lead arm and keeping it under throughout the swing. Ruth taught it in baseball, and Sam Byrd brought it into golf, explained it to Hogan and some of the other guys. Sam Byrd found that in golf all the great players did it. Whether they knew did it or not, they did it, just like the great hitters all do it." Jimmy Ballard.

While living in San Diego, this author took a golf lesson from John Schlee, the third round leader and eventual runner up to Johnnie Miller when he posted his final round 64 in the 1973 US Open. Imagine how that impacted Schlee's life. Schlee, who was one of the chosen few to spend time on the lesson tee with Hogan in Fort Worth. His message to me . . . "imagine holding an orange between your elbows."

"A word of emphasis about the elbows. You want to press them as closely together as you can. When you do this (and the elbows point directly to the hip bones) you will notice that the pocket of each elbow—the small depression on the inside of the joint—will lie in the center of the arm, at the midway point. The pockets will be facing toward the sky, as they should, not toward each other. In this position of address, though the left arm hangs relatively straight, the right arm should be broken a little at the elbow as the elbow points in. The right elbow, as it folds close to the body, should always be pointing toward the ground. If the upper part of the right arm adheres as closely as possible to the side of the chest." Ben Hogan.

"As your arms become schooled, you will get the feeling that the arms and the club form one firm unit—sort of as if the two arms were equal sides of a triangle, with the club emerging like the spire of a steeple at the peak point where the arms join." Ben Hogan.

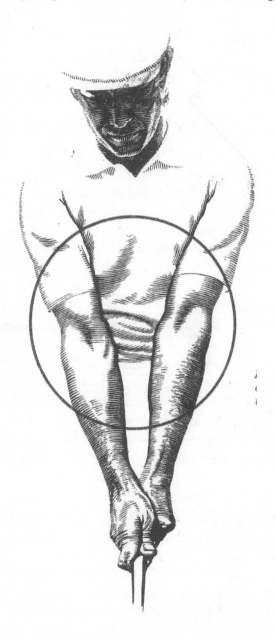

Lower Body: Stance, Posture, Ball Position

"The value of perfect posture and body rhythm." Walter Hagen.

"Never reach for the ball. Your weight as you address the ball should be distributed evenly between the ball and the heel of each foot, with special emphasis on the left foot. This gives you the best possible foundation for your swing. If you start reaching perceptibly for the ball, the arc of your swing will become to flat. The predominant fault is standing too far from the ball, rather than too close to it. It is next to impossible to stand too close to the ball." Byron Nelson.

"Many a golfer make the sizable error of thinking of the stance as that preparatory part of the swing in which the player merely lines himself up on the target he or she is shooting at. While one of the purposes of the stance certainly is to set up the direction of the shot, it also has quite a number of other functions that are much more important. Power and control must be combined in a good golf swing, and the stance is that step in which a golfer sets himself up so that (1) his body will be in balance throughout the swing, (2) his/her muscles are ready to perform fluidly, and (3) as a logical result, all the energy he pours into his swing will be channeled to produce maximum control and power. When you see a fine player making little individual movements of his feet or his knees or his shoulders as he settles into his stance, do not mistake these for empty gestures of nervousness. And they're not movements, either, that precede his arriving at a static, fixed position. What he's actually trying to do is to *feel* that everything he will be calling on in his swing is in balance and poised for action." Ben Hogan.

"The feet should be set apart the width of the shoulders when you are playing the standard five iron shot. They are somewhat closer together when you play the more lofted clubs, somewhat wider than the width of the shoulders when you play the long irons and the woods." Ben Hogan

"You should bend your knees from the thighs down. As your knees bend, the upper part of the trunk remains erect, just as it does when you sit down in a chair. In golf, the sit down motion is more like lowering yourself onto a spectator-sports-stick. Think of the seat of the seat as being about two inches or so below your buttocks.

In this semi-sitting position, your body should feel in balance both laterally and back to front. You should feel a sense of heaviness in your buttocks. There should be more tension in your legs from the knees down - the lower part of your legs should feel very springy and strong, loaded with elastic energy. Your weight should be a bit more on the heels than on the balls of your feet, so that, if you wanted to, you would be able to lift your toes inside of your shoes. The back remains as naturally erect as it is when you're walking down a fairway. Do not crouch the shoulders over the ball. You bend your head down only by bending your neck, not your back or shoulders." Ben Hogan.

"You know why I'm so goddam good? I never move my right knee." Ben Hogan to his caddy

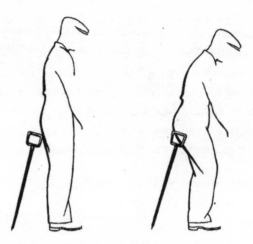

*The sit-down motion is like lowering yourself
(about two inches) onto a spectator-sports-stick*

*Numerous average golfers
fail to realize that an
incorrect stance and faulty
posture greatly affect
the success of the entire
swing. The golfer is off
balance from the start if he
keeps his legs stiff, or lets
his knees buckle, or
crouches his shoulders
way over the ball*

The proper stance and posture enable a golfer to be perfectly balanced and poised throughout the swing. Only then will his legs, arms, and body be able to carry out their interrelated assignments correctly

Ball Position

"The basic objective in positioning the ball is to where the path of the descending clubhead momentarily coincides with the target line. Although down through the years many good players have used one ball position for all basic shots - I believe Byron Nelson and Ben Hogan both did - others have preferred to move the ball about in relations to the feet depending on the club being used. However, the trend among modern tournaments players is to position the ball identically for every standard shot. I play every standard shot with the ball in the same position relative to my feet. The position should be opposite my left heel." Jack Nicklaus

Alignment

If you watch any footage of Jack Nicklaus hitting a golf shot, he always picked out an intermediary target as he began his setup. "I would find a leaf or some sort of mark on the grass on the target line a few feet ahead of the ball and in my mind's eye 'see' a line connecting the ball and my mark line up the clubface while looking from behind the ball through my mark to the target; then, holding the clubface in position, walk around it and align myself in an address position square to the face." Jack Nicklaus.

Shoulder Alignment Governs Path of Clubhead

"Whatever alignment you seek at address—open, square, or closed—don't make the mistake thinking that by aligning your feet one way your body will automatically follow. The critical alignment factor is the shoulders. Remember that, unless you make a deliberate effort not to, you instinctively swing the club through the ball parallel to your shoulders, no matter where your feet may be aligned." Jack Nicklaus.

All golfers have a dominant eye. Generally speaking, it's the right eye. If you elect not to pick out an intermediary target in the initial phase of the setup, you run the risk of opening your shoulders—ever so slightly—every time you look at your target. This is one aspect of the setup that all students of the game should incorporate into their routines. Picking out an intermediary target and aligning your shoulders (not your feet) parallel to that target. If you hit a slice, there is a high probability that you have your shoulders open in the alignment phase of the set up.

As Jack Nicklaus said, "Shoulder alignment governs path of the clubhead. You will instinctively swing the club through the ball parallel to your shoulders, no matter where your feet may be aligned." With an intermediary target, you eliminate the dominant eye, nudging the shoulders ever so open every time you peer at the target.

----------------------------- shoulders, hips, knees, feet

----------------------------- line of flight TARGET

Waggling

"As ye waggle so shall ye swing." old Scottish adage.

"Waggle spontaneously." Walter Hagen.

"At the moment you stand ready to hit the ball there is a natural tendency to tighten up in your hands, wrists, arms, and shoulders. I have found the most effective means of overcoming this tension is the waggle—abbreviated, easy, loose, back and forth movement with the clubhead. To derive maximum benefit, make these preliminary loosening-up motions in the line-of-flight in which you intend to hit the shot. The manner which you waggle you have a definite bearing on the way you start the clubhead back for the swing. Avoid waggling too much. This defeats the purpose of the waggle." Byron Nelson.

"The essence of rhythmic swing is to be smooth, for only the smooth swing can be rhythmic. But if you get undue clubhead agitation into your preparatory movement (which is what the waggle is) you will get all the feel in your hands, arms, and shoulders, not in your legs, hips, and back, which is where you should feel that you swing from." Byron Nelson.

"Then the waggle. About the waggle a whole book could be written. Every movement we make when we waggle is a miniature of the swing we intend to make, The clubhead moves in response to the body and the body opposes the clubhead. It is a flow and counter flow of forces with no static period, no check. There is no check anywhere in a good swing. There is no such thing as the "dead top" of a swing . . . the waggle—which is the bottom of an imaginary swing! Because unless you feel the whole of the swing in your waggle, your waggle is failing in its purpose. The whole meaning and purpose of the waggle is that you shall first feel your swing rightly so that you may then make it rightly. I remember watching Sand Herd make his first Cine pictures. In order not to waste film he tried to do without his customary fourteen waggles (shades of Sergio Garcia) and in consequence he could not hit the ball. He could not make the shot because he had not felt it." Percy Boomer

"Unless you feel the whole of the swing in your waggle, your waggle is failing in its purpose." Percy Boomer.

"The main thing to remember is that the waggle is just a little bitty swing that follows along the same path—for maybe a foot or so—that your full swing will travel. The waggle sets the tempo for the whole swing, so that if you're ever fidgety and jerky with this movement, it's going to be difficult for you to make a smooth swing." Byron Nelson.

"If you do waggle, let the action help you preview the shot you're going to play by waggling along the desired swing path thus, out-to-in waggles for a fade and in-to-out waggles for a draw." Jack Nicklaus.

"Hogan," wrote Cary Middlecoff, "placed more emphasis on the waggle than any swing theorist before." He pointed out that Hogan himself had first become aware in 1932 of how crucial the waggle was when he observed the advantage Johnny Revolta gained by using it for short shots around the green. Hogan elaborated on this idea and applied it to his complete game.

"The bridge between the setup and the actual start of the back-swing is the waggle. As a golfer looks at his objective and figures out the kind of shot he is going to play, his instincts take over: he waggles the club back and forth. Many golfers have the mistaken idea that it doesn't really matter how you waggle the club. They think the only purpose in waggling the club is to loosen yourself up so that you won't be tense or rigid. The waggle is an extremely important part of shot making. Far from being just a lot of minute details, it is sort of miniature practice swing and abbreviated "dry run" for the shot coming up. As the golfer takes the club back on the waggle, he accustoms himself to the path of the club he will be taking on his actual backswing." Ben Hogan

"The rhythm of the waggle varies with each shot you play. Don't groove your waggle. It takes instinct to plan and play a golf shot, and your preparations for each shot must be done instinctively. Let's say, for example, that you're 130 yards out from a semi plateau green. You've decided that you want to get the ball well up in the air in a steep trajectory, and that you'll be playing a seven-iron. You want to strike the shot firmly, but you want to hit a soft, feathery kind of shot that will float down onto the green. The waggle will be somewhat slowly, somewhat softly. This is the tempo you will also be using on the stroke, of course. Say, on the other hand, that you've got to bang a drive low into the wind on a hole where it's important to be out a good distance from the tee to get home in two. For this shot, you'll move the club back and forth with much more briskness, more conviction, more speed, and you'll swing that way. The waggle, in other words, fit's the shot." Ben Hogan

The common denominator among better golfers is that they waggle consistently, instinctively, and they do it on every shot.

An exaggerated long waggle in which Hogan demonstrates that he likes to feel the clubface open.

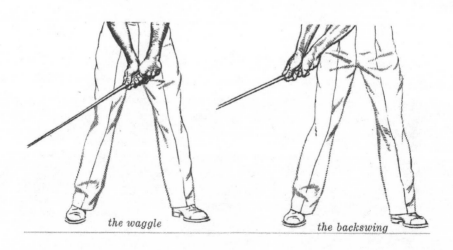

the waggle   *the backswing*

II. Swing

Takeaway

There are a couple of schools of thought regarding the takeaway. John Geertsen Sr. advocated "setting the angle early" as opposed to what Lucious Bateman taught, the one-piece takeaway (more about that in Lessons from the Six Under Par Club). In a one-piece takeaway, when your hands are at hip level, the club shaft is parallel to the ground. In "setting the angle early" takeaway, when your hands are at hip level, the club shaft is perpendicular to the ground. Johnny Miller's ("find an angle and keep it") record speaks for itself as what can be accomplished with an early set. For the average player—an early set has a tendency to activate the hands too soon in the golf swing. At the time of Johnny's success, this methodology became very controversial. Hogan, Snead, Lord Byron, Palmer, Nicklaus (to name but a few) all employed a "one-piece takeaway."

Many golf instructors advocate early angle setting somewhere between the takeaway and when the hands reach hip level. For those, if there isn't a shoulder turn along with the angle set, it activates the hands. Instead of keeping the hands passive, they become active. Once the hands are "activated," the triangle (both hands on the grip of the club connected to your shoulders) "separates," and the hands get ahead of the body. Once this happens, power is displaced, and the ball can go anywhere—usually a relatively short distance. By turning the triangle (billiard rack) with the big muscles (shoulders) and getting your left arm and hand extended out and in control, you're able to capture the feeling of a true pivot. This is not to say that an early angle set is wrong. The student who adheres to the "early set" methodology needs to realize it is imperative to keep the angle behind the body while initiating the downswing.

"There is no action in golf less understood than the use of the wrists, for curiously enough we do not have to work them, but we have to let them work themselves—like hinges on a door." Percy Boomer.

In support of a one piece takeaway.

"The triangle formed by our arms and a line between the shoulders should never lose its shape . . . it should be possible to push a wooden snooker triangle in between the arms and to leave it there without impeding the swing back or through." Percy Boomer.

"The wrists cock themselves. If you hold your wrists free to respond to the movement of the swing and to the momentum of the clubhead which sets up that movement, the weight of the clubhead itself will be sufficient to cock the wrists for you." Percy Boomer.

"At no time make a conscious effort to cock the wrists. By this I am not saying there is no cocking of the wrists. It is the deliberate attempt to do so that causes looseness in your swing—and this is a severe detriment to accuracy and consistency." Byron Nelson.

"When you swing back to waist high—the shaft parallel to the ground—the toe of the club must be pointed straight up to the sky." Harvey Penick.

"The wrist cock is an integral part of the backswing, and should not be cultivated as an independent action." Sam Snead.

"I believe that you cannot start the club back too slowly, provided you swing it back rather than take it away from the ball. I said in a previous book that the ideal swing start is a terribly forced, ridiculously slow movement of the club away from the ball. I still feel that way. The harder I want to swing, the slower I try to start the club back. But on every shot, I endeavor to swing the club in motion very deliberately, very positively, only just fast enough to avoid jerkiness. Obviously, the motion speeds up as my backswing develops, but the slower I can keep those first few feet of the takeaway, the better I'll play. Reasons? Primarily three: (1) The slower you start back, the better chance of moving the clubhead on a particular line, and thus the better your chance of establishing the particular arc and plane you desire. (2) The slower you start back, the easier it is to coordinate or unify the movements of the feet, legs, hips, hands, arms, and shoulders, the better your chance of starting back in one piece. (3) The slower you start back—while still swinging the club, mind you - the smoother the over-all tempo you'll establish." Jack Nicklaus.

"I once heard Arnold Palmer say that if he got started right away during the first 14 inches of his swing he never had to think about anything else during the rest of it. That may be a slight exaggeration, particularly for a player who has less ability than Arnold, but it illustrates the importance good players place on the takeaway. I believe that your takeaway should be one piece. You should feel that you are starting the club back with your whole left side moving together with your left hand and arm. When I was playing my best, I definitely began my takeaway with my left side. The left hand is firmly in control. The left shoulder and left arm push the club away from the ball on a straight line for a few inches, then swing it into the air. The relaxed right side is just pushed out of the way." Byron Nelson.

"The clubhead is placed at the back of the ball, and the swing commences so slowly in as to suggest that it is indolent." Bobby Jones.

"The two danger points are at the start of the backswing and the start of the down stroke. To start back smoothly avoids haste later on; to start down in a leisurely fashion helps to maintain the perfect balance, and provides for well-timed, accurate striking." Bobby Jones.

"The initial movement of the club away from the ball should result from forces originating in the left side. The real takeoff is from the left foot, starting movement of the body. The hands and arms very soon pick it up, but the proper order at the beginning is body, arms, and lastly clubhead. It is always easier to continue a motion than to begin it: this order has the virtue of originating the hip-turn; it goes a long way toward assuring a proper windup of the hips during the backswing." Bobby Jones.

"I just try to do it the most simplest way I know how. I don't bother thinking about it; what I do is just take the club back nice and lazy and then try to whop it right down on the barrelhead." Sam Snead.

"When I'm trying for an extra-long drive, I actually feel I am taking the club back more deliberately, not with more strength." Sam Snead.

"Footwork, balance, is everything to me because of my life long theory (and Ben Hogan agreed) that the more you minimize hand, wrist and arm action, the better. I believe the body pivot launched by the feet is the big factor." Sam Snead.

"If your feet transfer all your weight to the right side easily, your hips turn, and your shoulders will follow. Don't ever separate the action of your hands, arms, and shoulders. It's easy to do without realizing it: Hands and shoulders must work together, but the shoulders take the lead." Sam Snead.

"Then from about 1937 on through the rest of my career, I didn't think about much while making a shot. I had developed a style of play which I used all through this period. It became pretty automatic and effortless. I had a target in mind and I just visualized the line on which I wanted to take the club away from the ball, and the line on which I wanted to return it. That was the thought the triggered my swing." Sam Snead.

"If he executes his backswing properly, as his arms are approaching hip level, they should be parallel with the plane and they should remain parallel with the plane, just beneath the glass...." Ben Hogan.

"To accomplish an efficient swing we have to build a mental picture of the path we want the clubhead to follow, from address to the top of the backswing and down again—sort of a road map of the swing. And to put the clubhead on this path we have to start by taking it back low and along a perfectly straight line for at least a full foot. Why? Because you want to bring the clubhead back along the same track when you hit the ball. Remember those two points above all: Picture the path of the swing in your mind, and start the club back along that path. These are the keystones in the structure of the swing. Start the club back smooth and silky." Tony Lema.

One-piece takeaway versus angle setting . . . in these three photos the shoulders have turned about the same, the hands are slightly above hip level; however, the shaft angle to the ground is different.

Staying on Plane throughout the Backswing

"Timing and hesitation at the top of the swing." Walter Hagen.

"When your forward shoulder hits your chin, you're pretty much done with the backswing. Don't try for more than this. It's been said that Ben Hogan used to wear out his shirt at the point of the left shoulder because his backswing was so consistent that the same spot always hit his chin. He must have had a tough beard! Of course, he hit an awful lot of balls, too. The trigger for me was pinning that left shoulder up against the chin. Once I got there, I knew I was done with my backswing. Anything else after that was a wasted motion that bred inconsistency." Johnny Miller.

"Turning the left shoulder underneath your chin on the backswing. Get a feel of getting your left shoulder underneath your chin. Once your shoulders stop—your hands stop." John McMullen.

"Visualize the backswing plane as a large pane of glass that rests on the shoulders as it inclines upward for the ball. As the arms approach hip level on the backswing, they should be moving parallel with the plane and should remain parallel with the plane (just below the glass) to the top of the backswing. It would be ideal if the arms could be swung back parallel to the plane from the very start of the swing, but because of the way we human beings are constructed, a man gripping a club can't get his arm onto the plane until they are nearly hip high." Ben Hogan.

"The center of gravity of the body must stay in one place throughout the swing. That is, if a line is drawn through the nose or head to the ground, the head must stay in that position throughout the swing." Ben Hogan.

"By simply trying to turn the top of my left shoulder underneath my chin on the backswing I was finally able to achieve a sensation at the top of my backswing." I. B. Nobody.

A checkpoint for a proper shoulder turn is that you should feel the left shoulder brushing your chin at the top of the backswing.

Illus 7-12
Seymour Dunn was an innovative teacher from a famous family of golf professionals. Here he demonstrates the plane angles' degree of steepness.

Illus 7-13
Here Dunn demonstrates how the butt of the club points to the plane's baseline.

The Plane.
Backswing plane
inclines upward from the
ball through the shoulders.
As arms approach hip level
on backswing, they should
be moving parallel with
the plane and should remain
parallel with the plane
throughout the backswing

Initiating the Downswing

"The trunk muscles are the most powerful muscles of the body." Bobby Jones.

"The only one who has a chance to achieve a rhythmic, well-timed stroke is the man who, in spite of all else, yet swings his club-head, and the crucial area is where the swing changes direction at the top. If the backswing can be made to flow back leisurely, and to an ample length, from where the start downward can be made without the feeling that there may not be enough time left, there is a good chance of success." Bobby Jones.

"It is the leisurely start downward which provides for a gradual increase of speed without disturbing the balance and the timing of the swing." Bobby Jones.

"As the downswing begins, one should have the feeling of leaving the clubhead at the top." Bobby Jones.

"I should say the most important movement of the swing would be to start the downswing by beginning the unwinding of the hips. . . there can be no power, and very little accuracy or reliability, in a swing in which the left hip does not lead the down stroke." Bobby Jones.

"No matter how perfect the backswing may have been, if the hands, or the arms, or the shoulders start the downward movement, the club immediately loses the guidance of the body movement, and the benefit of the power the muscles of the waist and back could have contributed. When this happens, the turn of the body during the backswing becomes entirely useless, and the club finds itself in midair, actuated by a pair of hands and arms having no effective connection with anything solid. I think we may well call this the most important movement of the swing." Bobby Jones.

"And we will fail to drive the ball far and straight as soon as we fail to take control of the club from the top of the swing with feet, calves, and thighs." Percy Boomer.

"So we must incorporate into our swings a hip movement which we can recognize and control by a definite feel, so that by feel we may control the degree and direction of power in our swings. The clutch in the golfer's mechanism is the hips . . . ." Percy Boomer.

"The power is largely produced by the feet and legs, but it is the force-center (somewhere in the pit of the back), which collects it and is responsible for its transfer to the arms and then out to the clubhead." Percy Boomer.

"The left hip, with the right immediately joining it, leads me into the downswing." Sam Snead.

"It slowed me down, and this time I remembered, on my downswing, to let my left side and hips lead my arms into the ball - rather than rushing out of my pivot with a fast arm action—and to uncock my wrists smoothly." Sam Snead.

"It is important that this be a well-timed sequence. You should have the feeling that the left foot, left knee, left hip and left shoulder all start the downswing together. This leading left side then carries the left arm and hands down into the hitting area. The clubhead is being returned to its original position, ready to be released by the hands and wrists at the proper time." Byron Nelson.

"Feeling leisurely is a thought that worked. In my earlier days, I developed what felt like a complete hesitation. It was very brief, and I probably never did come to a full stop at the top. So the smoother and slower you can be at the very top of the swing, and then starting down, the better you'll strike the ball." Byron Nelson.

"The hips initiate the downswing. They are the pivotal element in the chain action. Starting them first and moving them correctly - this action practically makes the downswing. It creates early speed. It transfers the weight from the right foot to the left foot. It takes the hips out of the way and gives your arms plenty of room to pass. It funnels your force forward toward your objective. It puts you in a strong hitting position where the big muscles in the back and the muscles in the shoulders, arms and hands are properly delayed that they can produce their maximum performance at the right time and place. To begin the downswing, *Turn your hips back to the left. there must be enough lateral motion forward to transfer the weight to the left foot.*" Ben Hogan.

"If you clear the left hip early." Hogan once assured Claude Harmon, "you can hit it as hard as you like with the right hand."

"To start the downswing the left hip bumps the target, then turns through the shot." Claude Harmon.

"You start the downswing by unwinding from the ground up."
Jack Nicklaus.

Check out the position of the knees and right foot in the photos on left vs. the photos on right. The hands are being led into impact by the lower body. Shades of MacDonald Smith: "Hit it with the butt end of the club."

Hitting Through in One Cohesive Movement

"The ordinary golfer is an unrepentant end-gainer. When he sees the ball, he becomes obsessed with the idea of hitting it; the ball is made the climax or the end of his activity." Percy Boomer.

"Because it is no use trying to write an intelligent book on golf and leaving rhythm out, for rhythm is the very soul of golf . . . and the best definition I know of it is, co-ordination of mind and muscle which enables the player to do exactly the right thing at the proper moment. So you must find your own rhythm." Percy Boomer.

"Timing, then, is (1) The gathering of speed through the ball from correct mechanical movement and (2) a correct conception of the location of the swing center. These two can only be blended into a whole which can be faithfully repeated time after time by our sense of rhythm." Percy Boomer.

"Golf rhythm is a delayed dragging feel of the clubhead, developed from the power of the legs, kept under control by the braced turning of the hips, and finally loosened into a free, untrammeled movement of the arms outward and around the left side. We lose rhythm as soon as we hurry, and we hurry as soon as we are afraid." Percy Boomer.

"As I have said before, the swing is a continuous unbroken movement that cannot be cut into sections for analysis." Percy Boomer.

"Always remember that your swing does not end at clubhead impact with the ball. You must hit completely through. The ball is hit from impact on through, and not to the ball. This holds true for all clubs. My hands are still firmly in control of the club at the finish of the swing. The supposition that the eyes must remain fixed throughout the follow through on the spot from which the ball was hit is completely erroneous. This is unnatural and retards the free and full turn of the shoulders." Byron Nelson.

"The difference between swinging hard and over swinging was a big one for me. At 100 percent of powers, hitches appeared in the transference of weight from left to right and back again. The only time I dared hit flat out—with everything I had—came on the unusual occasion when I felt perfectly balanced and my timing was exact. Experimenting again with shoes off, I found that I naturally cut down until I was using just the right medium of swing, or about

85 or 90 percent of full power, without thinking twice about it. The reason was that a man won't over swing if he doesn't have spikes gripping the turf for him. Barefoot, your nerves are exposed to the ground. You're able to 'feel' balance, to judge how big a turn and windup is possible without disturbing the leverage of your body. You get that shade of restraint that counts." Sam Snead.

Slowing it down . . . "your problem is a swing that's too fast and jerky to be effective, there are a couple of things you can do to slow yourself down. First, slow down your breathing. Breathe a little deeper. You'll catch yourself breathing particularly fast during moments of pressure on the course, and you'll have trouble making a good swing if that's happening. Calm down your breathing and you'll calm down your body. Another good antidote to quickness is to move your feet more slowly during the address and waggle. Make a deliberate effort to do this, and you'll find it one of the easiest and best ways in the world to slow your swing down." Byron Nelson.

"The movement of the hips inaugurates a whole chain of actions. Tied in with the hips, the left leg begins to break back to the left and the left knee turns a bit toward the target. Starting the hips back also takes the pressure off the right leg, and as this happens, the weight flows to the left leg. The right knee breaks in, definitely, toward the target, boosting the mounting velocity of the swing. This is, in truth, what each element does as it joins in the downswing. It adds its contribution to the multiplying speed generated by this cohesive movement of the body, legs and arms toward the target. This speed multiplies the golfer's power 10 times over. In the chain action of the swing, the shoulders and upper part of the body conduct this multiplying power into the arms . . . the arms multiply it again and pass it on to the hands . . . The hands multiply it in turn tearing through the air at an incredible speed as it drives through the ball. All this happens so quickly, of course, that you can't see it to appreciate it. But this is what happens. The hips lead the shoulders all the way on the downswing. The shoulders finally catch up with the hips at the end of the swing." Ben Hogan.

Ernest Jones

The "swing the club head method," a simplified strategy for teaching the golf swing, originated with Ernest Jones of Great Britain in the early 20th century. Jones's philosophy was based on his belief that a golf swing involves one motion -- a unified whole rather than a series of parts. He said the golfer must feel the swinging motion through the hands; hence his mantra: "swing the club head." He eventually conducted his clinics at an office on the corner of Fifth Avenue and 43rd Street in Manhattan and became known as the Pro from Fifth Avenue.

The swing-the-club-head method is based on universal laws of science and simple logic. Jones believed that a golf swing should involve the club head moving in a simple back-and-forth manner, similar to a clock's pendulum or a child moving on a swing. In a 1949 article, Jones compared a golf swing to a circle, saying the shape is "simply one line, perfectly round. And it is just the same with a swing. A swing is one continuous motion, to and fro, backward and forward. Focusing on swinging the club with the intention of *creating centrifugal force* (my italics) in the club that could in turn propel the ball." He often demonstrated the motion to students by swinging a penknife tied to a handkerchief. Jones often said, "The trouble with the teaching of golf, is that one is taught what a swing produces [body movement], instead of how to produce a swing [club movement]."

Bobby Jones -- no relation to Ernest -- approved of the technique, saying, "We in the PGA picture tend to take a swing apart and divided into parts, but we know you can't teach it that way."

One of Ernest Jones's most notable students, Alister MacKenzie, says of Jones, "Ernest Jones is perhaps the world's most successful teacher."

Kenny Venturi

Many long years ago on the first tee of La Rinconada Country Club in Los Gatos, I. B. witnessed Ken Venturi giving a clinic before a Catholic Charity golf event. By happenstance, the author was practicing his short game around the putting green when the 1964 US

Open Champ appeared to conduct the clinic. Venturi was there at the request of one of the bishops of the Catholic church. Venturi, a deeply religious man, reminisced about the lessons he had taken from Byron Nelson.

Being in the right place at the right time, and listening attentively to what he had to say about how Byron stressed the importance of a full shoulder turn, and finishing in a balanced position. He told us how he worked for hours, "you open the spring" (turning his left shoulder underneath his chin) "and you close the spring" (turning all the way through until his right shoulder touched his chin). He encouraged us to attempt to incorporate that thought—that feel—into our games. An epiphany—it hit me like a ton of bricks—this was a feel that Venturi practiced to perfection . . . and an abstract that became symbol for movement once that feel became muscle memory.

In golf as in life, it's the follow-through that makes the difference.

Walter Hagen

Some of Walter Hagen's thoughts about the swing:

Even keel - rhythm, footing, and balance vs. jerky, gear shifting movement.

Feel for timing.

But at all times keeping my eye focused on the ball.

I like to hit the ball very firmly.

You must keep your mind completely on the shot to be made.

Hold my breath and let one go,

Trying to preserve rhythm.

Allow the wind to help it along.

Down the pretty

And one from his traveling companion . . . "Tempo, rhythm, timing, whatever you want to call it, is the great intangible ingredient of an outstanding swing. Convince yourself that the club doesn't need that much help from you." Joe Kirkwood.

III. Impact

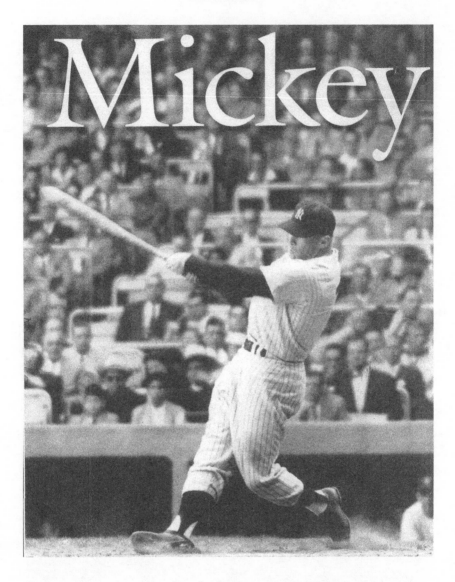

Mickey

"By crucial strokes played with imagination and precision when anything ordinary would not have sufficed. And I think I was able to do this because I had learned so well what golf ball could be made to do and how it had to be struck to make it perform as I wanted it to . . . I watched other players, too, and when one of them made a shot that I especially admired, I would begin to try to produce the same result. But I didn't observe how they took the club back or measure the body-turn they used. I watched the clubface strike the ball and saw how the ball responded. Then I tried to make my ball do the same thing. I think the average golfer would present a more natural appearance if he should put his mind upon striking the ball, rather than upon swinging the club. This knowledge will make you a better player overnight. If you are wary of being told to concentrate without having any knowledge of what you should concentrate on, this is it . . . Golf is played by striking the ball with the head of the club. The objective of the player is not to swing the club in a specific manner, nor to execute a series of complicated movements in a prescribed sequence, nor to look pretty while he is doing it, but primarily and essentially to strike the ball with the head of the club so that the ball will perform according to his wishes . . . These are the basic conceptions which should be in the golfer's mind every time he looks at a ball in preparation for playing a shot. He must have decided where he wants the ball to go. He should have a picture in his mind of the flight he hopes to produce, and then he must swing his club with the very definite and determined intention of having the clubhead meet the ball in such a way. This should be the object of his intense concentration. I should like to propose at this point that the reader obtain a golf ball and any sort of lofted iron club and begin straightaway to fix these concepts in his mind. In his own living room he can place the face of the club behind the ball, and without swinging, visualize the spinning effects which must result from the various kinds of contacts. It is in this very way that a player should approach every shot he hits on the golf course, or even on the practice tee . . . One may very easily and with great advantage carry this thing one step further. Indeed, for the best in performance, the player must keep in the forefront of his mind throughout the entire stroke this very clear picture of the precise manner in which he intends to strike the ball." Bobby Jones.

"Above all, he should be convinced that he cannot lift the ball from a cuppy or downhill lie by striking upward; on the contrary, he must rely upon backspin to cause the ball to become airborne." Bobby Jones.

"One important fact to keep in mind as we consider the technique of playing shots with the irons is that the ball is struck with a descending blow. In other words, the bottom of the arc of the swing comes slightly forward of the position in which the ball lies. This means the sole of the blade or clubhead cuts down into the turf after initial clubface impact with the ball." Byron Nelson.

"The ultimate judge of your swing is the flight of the ball." Ben Hogan.

"I let results impose form on my swing, rather than theory or style or any other factor." Sam Snead.

Johnnie Miller was asked, "Was there a particular part of the golf swing that you emphasized in your practice sessions?" "Yes that segment would be the moment of impact. My study of the swing revolved around impact because, ultimately, impact is all that really matters. I used to practice 'image' impact and 'feel' impact—lots of people say you can't do that, but in my prime, I could feel impact. I felt like I could almost stop at impact and tell exactly where my hands were at the moment, the position of the knees, everything. That was the reason why, I think, and other people say, I was the best iron player ever. I think it was because I had this belief that impact was possible to get a grasp of it. It wasn't just a blur."

"A perfectly straight shot with a big club is a fluke." Jack Nicklaus.

One particular type of swing does not fit all, and you must build your theories and swing keys around your own needs and requirements. "Working from the ball back" is the ideal place to start developing your swing.

Not Getting Desired Impacts?
   * Great players are never too far away from being able to fade (slice) or draw (hook) the ball onto target.

How? By working from the ball back - the flight of the ball tells it all

What's that you say? You hit a draw when you wanted to hit a fade

1.   Check the face position at the top of your backswing - your grip could be either too strong (hook) or too weak (slice)

2. Check the outside rail of your divot - that will tell you about your shoulder alignment (the angle of the shoulders at address is the path of the clubhead)
3. Ball Position - too far forward or too far back
4. Your takeaway - too much on the inside or too much on the outside
* By knowing your swing
    you'll realize that some days you hit it shorter
    you'll know what's happening with your shot pattern
To change or correct & what follows is all good in the hood.

Transform words (specifics) into mental pictures (the subconscious does not understand English) then into feels. Close your eyes and use your kinesthetic sense.

The idea is to learn to hit better bad shots. The great Walter Hagen expected to hit six or seven bad shots in a round. Bobby Jones wrote that absolute consistency is impossible in golf. Hogan acknowledged that he only hit one or two shots that came off exactly as planned. The best players build their swings that produce playable misses—the fewer the misses, and the better the misses are, the more consistent a player becomes.

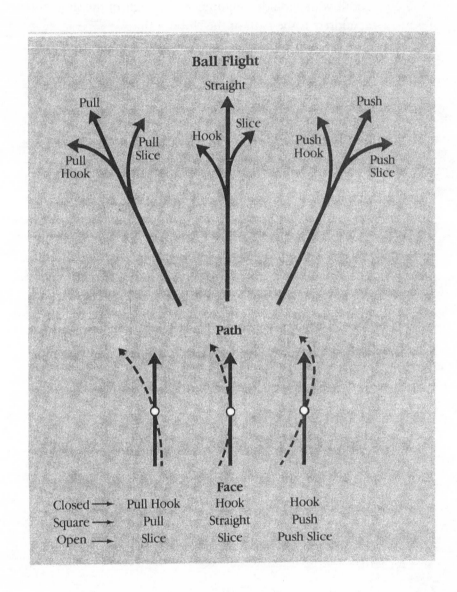

"A life is not important except in the impact it has on other lives" Jackie Robinson

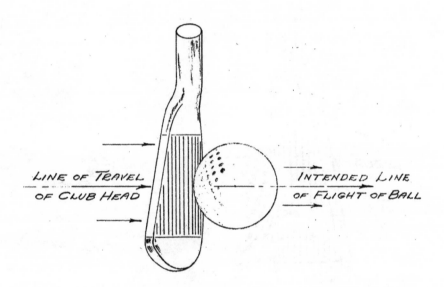

Figure 1. Plan View

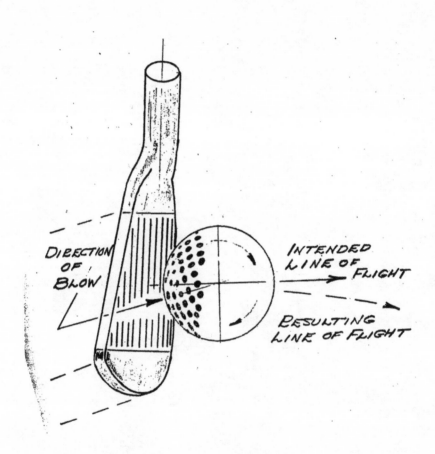

Figure 2. Slicing Contact

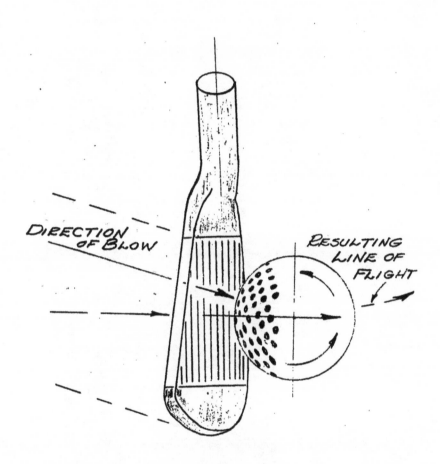

Figure 3. Hooking Contact

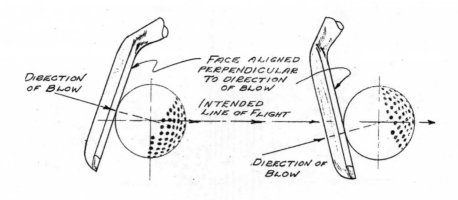

A Puch   Figure 4.   A Pull

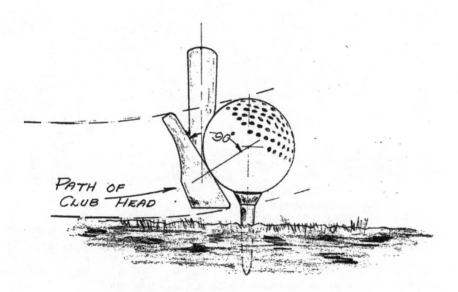

Figure 5. Striking the ball without producing backspin

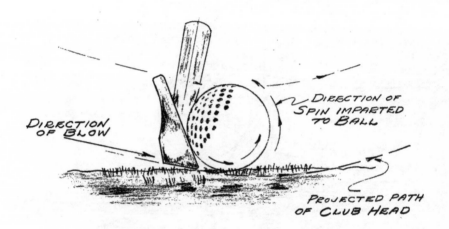

Figure 6. Producing backspin with a lofted iron.

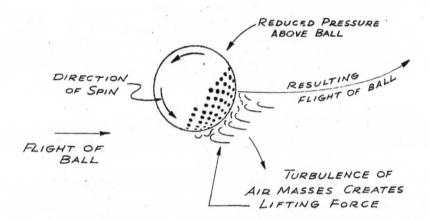

Figure 7. Side view of ball in fight, showing effect of backspin.

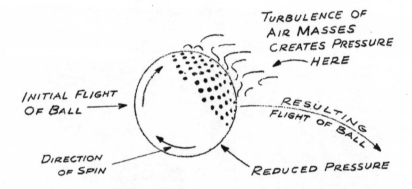

Figure 8. Looking down on ball in flight
showing effect of slicing spin.

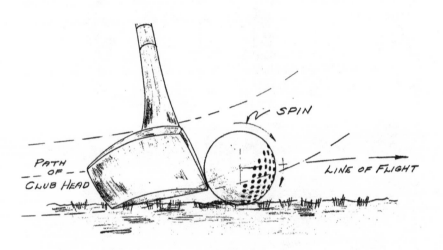

Figure 9. Wrong Way: improper upword stroke, improper spin.

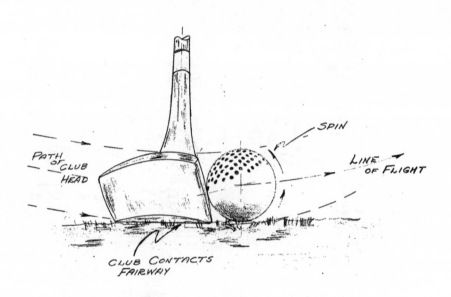

Figure 10. Right Way_ proper club loft, proper spin.

The Short Game

"Three of these and one of those still make four." Walter Hagen.

"The secret of golf is turning three shots into two." Bobby Locke.

"I want you to feel your hands only as a connecting link in the whole mechanism, not as a separate working part. Try to play a short chip shot guiding it and giving it its power entirely from your knees. When you can do that you will know what it is to feel connected." Percy Boomer.

"The short shot played with a delicate lob is the most effective scoring shot in golf." Percy Boomer.

"The two most important rules to observe are, first, to pitch over the intervening fairway or rough onto the putting surface whenever possible; and second, to play a straight forward shot without backspin whenever possible." Bobby Jones.

"In other words, when sizing up the shot, let the player ask himself a few questions in this order:

Is there room between the edge of the green and the flag for me to pitch to the green with a normal shot? If so, with what club? If not, can I pitch to the green with backspin and stop the ball quickly enough? If I can, will that shot be more risky than running the ball with a straight faced club over the intervening ground?" Bobby Jones.

On pitching . . . "The proper order of procedure is to visualize the shot, to determine where the pitch should drop and how much roll it should have; then to select the club and attempt the shot that should produce the result." Bobby Jones.

"Most good golfers are great chippers." Bobby Jones.

"It is demonstrably more difficult to control a shot with a club of extreme loft than with one of moderate pitch. Therefore, the clubs of extreme loft should be left in the bag until the need for them becomes well defined." Bobby Jones.

"One should avoid a quick stopping shot except when it is absolutely necessary." Bobby Jones.

"The turning of the body and shoulders and the use of the legs should be the same as in any other stroke. Indeed, it is my feeling that it is, if anything, more important here than elsewhere, to swing the clubhead. The swing should be leisurely, of ample length, and with a perceptible crispness as the ball is struck." Bobby Jones.

"Many golfers add unnecessary complexity to the game by feeling that they must use a different swing for each club in the bag. This is incorrect. Actually there is a slight variation in swing from one club differently than another. The natural variation is caused by the different positions in which you must stand to hit the ball for greater variety of lies encountered on any course, and the range of shaft lengths and clubhead angles. I am completely unaware of making any attempt to swing one club differently than another." Byron Nelson.

"In studying the finish of the swing you will see that it is necessary to swing completely through on every shot, regardless of the length of backswing may have been." Byron Nelson.

"Jones complimented my long hitting but remarked, "Distance is fine, accuracy is better. Be sure to take an inventory of your whole game, Sam. Do that after every round, with particular attention to how your close shots come off." Sam Snead.

"To be able to scramble from trouble, I want to repeat, is the key to winning golf. A lot of what I picked up as a green kid come from watching masters of the sand irons, such as Henry Cotton of England, Ralph Guldahl, Jimmy Demaret, Walter Hagen, Denny Shute, and Johnny Revolta." Sam Snead.

"Try to play a short chip guiding it and giving it its power entirely with the knees." Art Bell.

Here's a concept . . .

With a pitching wedge, your shoulders turn 90 degrees, your lower body leads the downswing, your hands and arms follow and the ball goes 100 yards.

* for a 50-yard shot – your shoulders turn 45 degrees, your lower body leads the the downswing, your hands and arms follow

* for a 25-yard shot – your shoulders turn 22.5 degrees, your lower body leads the downswing, your hands and arms follow

* for a 12.5-yard shot – your shoulders turn 11.25 degrees, your lower body leads the downswing, your hands and arms follow

* for a 6.25-yard shot – your shoulder turn 5.625 degrees, your lower body leads the downswing, your hands and arms follow

* for a 3.125-yard shot – your shoulders turn 2.81 degrees, your lower body leads the downswing, your hands and arms follow

What this translates to is that you are taking the same swing on every shot—just a shorter version. As the turn decreases, the weight moves from being balanced at address to 50 percent on your left side for the 45-degree shoulder turn. Then a little more on your left side on the 22.5-degree turn, to fully on your left side on the shortest of turns.

Once witnessed Gene Litler hitting a magnificent iron shot into the par 4 12th hole on the North Course at Silverado Country Club, hit a firm spot on the green that jumped into the back bunker. Now faced with a sand shot where the green was running away from him and the pin no more than fifteen feet away, he took what looked like a full swing—complete with his belly button facing the target at the finish of his swing—and the ball nestled down inches from the hole for a tap in par.

An actual occurrence . . . my first real caddy experience came in 1971 at the Kaiser International. Caddying for friends is one thing but this was tournament golf. The event was held at the Silverado Country Club in Napa, California. The first two rounds were played on the North and South courses—the players alternating courses— and after the 36 hole cut, the final two rounds were played on the North Course. Through Bateman, my loop was Dick Lotz. Because of his status as a tournament winner from the year prior, he was paired with the 1969 Masters champion, George Archer and the 1969 US Open champion, Orville Moody, for the first two rounds. In the first round, vividly remembering the 16th hole on the north course, a beautiful 5 par, margined on the left with a creek, (that runs the length of the hole) and two majestic oaks—one near the landing area of the tee shot and the other just to the right of the front of the green. Orville, playing with his persimmon driver, crafted a beautiful draw off the tee, 290 yards, right down the pretty. Gentleman George pull hooked his tee shot into the creek. Dick . . . down the pretty 275 yards in play. Second shots: Orville carved his three wood to the front edge of the green. George Archer dug his ball out of the creek and into the adjoining 14th fairway (a portion of the hole parallels the 16th). Dick Lotz hit his 3 wood 40 yards short of the green. Third shots: Orville lagged to four feet, George hit it over the trees into the bunker, Dick Lotz wedge to 6 feet. Fourth shots: George blasts out of the bunker to 3 feet. Dick Lotz holed his 6 footer for birdie, Orville missed his 4 footer. 5th shots: George makes his 3 footer, Orville tapped in for 5. George Archer probably made more pars in this fashion than anybody whose ever played the game. If the old adage, "The secret of golf is turning three shots into two," then George was the poster boy. Orville struck the ball as well as humanly possible and George chipped and putted his way to happiness. George played the way all great players play when strategizing how to play a golf hole—they work from the hole back and leave themselves makeable putts.

After rounds of 67/70, our third round pairing was Billy Casper, the best player in the world at the time, (in the 1960s, five of the ten Vardon Trophies had Casper's name inscribed on them) and a promising tour rookie, Tom Watson—who had to play in the Monday qualifying round to get into the tournament proper (the all exempt system wasn't in place until 1983) Quite a threesome, Dick Lotz struggling to keep it together, the wide eyed mustachioed Tom Watson (68/68) on the slow rise to the pinnacle and Casper at the peak of perfection. Tal Smith had told me of Billy Casper's wizardry around the greens. In winning the 1959 US Open at Winged Foot, while playing the 217 yard par 3 third hole, Casper laid up each day with an iron, wedged on and sank the putt for a par . . . in all four rounds. Casper schooled 'em. Pragmatic, he'd learn the bad spots on the golf course and do anything to avoid hitting it there. Casper had a very wristy putting stroke. On the short ones, the putter head traveled back and forth in the shape of a U. No question, he hit down on the ball while putting. When pitching or chipping, much like George Archer, he kept the ball low around the greens. On the par 4 13th on the North Course, with the pin tucked in the far left corner of a forty-foot long green, Casper had missed his ball short. Pulling out his six iron, he nonchalantly pitched the ball on the front of the green and let the ball roll across the green inches from the hole. Like all great players, Casper kept the ball out of the throw up zone. The game is so much easier if you stay away from the three or four footers all day long. Lag putting, pitching and chipping to within inches are a common denominator amongst the great ones.

The next year, in the 1972 Kaiser Invitational, Orville played with Ross Randle (another caddie gig lined up through Bateman). We witnessed Orville hit 9 greens on the front side of the South Course—on eight of the holes he never had the ball outside of fifteen feet, the other, a par 5 he hit in two, and shot one over par! Golf is a game of how many not how.

Digressing for a moment . . . who is this Ross Randall guy anyway? A Bateman protégé, he played golf for San Jose State University and was the first recipient of the Ken Venturi scholarship award. A First-team Collegiate All-American in 1967, in a class of six that included PGA standouts Johnny Miller and Hale Irwin.

Ross served as an assistant golf professional at Winged Foot Golf Club, Mamaroneck, NY, under the tutelage of Claude Harmon, winner of the 1948 Masters, before joining the PGA tour where he competed for eight years. In 1979, he moved to Lawrence, Kansas and was part of the University of Kansas men's golf program for three decades, including 28 years as head coach. Ross guided seven KU teams to the NCAA Championships and 19 to NCAA Regionals. From 1981-1984 he doubled as both the women's and men's golf coach. In 1999, he took the fifth-seeded Jayhawks into the Big 12 Conference Championship and captured the program's first league title in 49 years. In 2014, he was inducted into the Kansas Golf Hall of Fame.

Digressing for another moment . . . whose this Dick Lotz guy anyway? Dick played on the PGA tour from 1964–1978. In 1970, he finished seventh on the year's official money list. He won three tour events (1969 Alameda Open, 1970 Kemper Open, 1970 Monsanto Open). As an amateur, in winning the 54 hole, 1963 Santa Clara County Championship, Dick bested his brother, John (who had shot three rounds in the 60s) by recording nary a round in the 60s but one in the 50s! A 59 on the par 70 San Jose Country Club! A course record (that still stands) may be equaled but certainly never broken. 11 birdies, no bogies. "Had a 12-footer on 18 for 59. Knew I was going to make it. Hell, I made everything that day." However, Dick did have one other claim to fame . . .

Hogan's Last Competitive Round

"The commonly held view is that Ben Hogan made his final public tournament appearance in the spring of 1971 when he magically appeared at Houston for a second time. After scoring four consecutive pars on the course's unremittingly long opening holes during the first round, the hobbling Hawk attempted to fade a low flying three iron shot into the front portion of the 190 yard par 3 4th hole and dumped his ball in a deep creek ravine that guarded the green. To the surprise of and then astonishment of his playing partners Dick Lotz and Charles Coody, and a gallery of Hogan loyalists who seemed to materialize every time he appeared in a public setting, Ben dropped two more balls on the spot and drilled them into Cypress Creek as well. To compound matters, while climbing down the slope to hunt for his wayward shots, his weak left knee buckled and he nearly toppled into the creek. With a limp that was noticeably more pronounced with every step, Hogan climbed out of the ravine and finished the hole with a woeful nine, completing his opening nine with a 44. Following a double bogey at 10 and a bogey at 11, his knee gave way again on the tee shot at 12, and he nearly spilled to the ground a second time. His ball lay in the fairway, though, and a few minutes later he sent it sailing over a small pond to the heart of the green, one fine farewell shot to a lifetime of competition. As if he had at least convinced himself he could still hit a couple decent golf shots," wrote his early biographer Gene Gregston. "Hogan called it a day and a career." He stood for a moment in the classic Hogan pose: hands on hips, white cap shading his eyes as his caddie walked

around the pond to pick up his ball. He turned to his playing partners and said, "I'm sorry, fellas. I'm through." A few minutes later,
Hogan climbed on a motorized cart and rode silently back to the
locker room with his head tilted down, the pose of defeat from so
long ago, a sad, ignominious ending to the most accomplished career
in professional golf."

Do you know that 60-65 percent of the shots in golf take place
within 90 yards of the hole? One should never forget to work on
his/her short game and develop it in tandem with your long game.
If you want to improve your scores, this is one area of the game that
requires a tremendous amount of practice but will reap dividends in
the scoring department. If you'll practice holding the "billiard rack"
in place and getting the force of the blow coming entirely from your
knees you'll improve your short game. Weight distribution is vital.
If you find yourself hitting behind the ball, you're either looking up
or your arms and hands are ahead of your body. An improved short
game is vital to any golfer's plan to reach his/her potential.

On the following page, pay particular attention to the action of
Fred Couples left hip . . . especially his left pants pocket

LOW VS. LOB

The best way to understand the soft, lofted chip is by seeing it side-by-side with the conventional chip shot. Both are about 25 yards long, carry plus roll.

Address. As shown on the facing page, the ball should be in the middle of your stance, weight evenly distributed between your feet, your hands and head in-line with the ball. This ensures that the club—one with loft, no lower than a 9-iron—slips under the ball, tossing it in the air.

Backswing. In the conventional chip, your wrists stay firm. The lob needs wrist break to create a U-shaped swing. It's important that your motion stays loose and flowing all the way back and through. Compare that to the tighter, more restricted look (and feel) of the low chip.

Impact and Follow-through. You can see how the club slides under the ball on the lobbed shot, then continues on and up, mirroring the U-shape of the backswing. Also notice the difference in leg action: The lower body is quiet during the low chip, but looser and more active on the lob (check the finish position of the right knee).

LOW RUNNING CHIP

Routines

Psycho-cybernetics is a subject that intrigues Johnnie Miller. He feels it is necessary to train the subconscious to overrule the conscious . . . that the subconscious is the overriding factor in your execution. "You don't try to change your muscle memory," he says. "Before the shot," adds Miller, "I visualize the flight of the ball and the type of swing I want to use . . . how the ball feels when it hit's the clubface and leaves the clubface, the trajectory of the shot, how it flies, how it lands on the green . . . This is programming your subconscious—programming the computer. Then all I've got to do is pick the club, get over the ball and . . . *bam!* I let my subconscious take over and it will hit the shot for me. "That's why it is so important to see yourself on videotape or movies or in a mirror, because if you don't have an exact idea of what your swing looks like you can't communicate with your subconscious. Of course, you must program a success," Miller warns. "You must visualize the shot going onto the green, the putt dropping in the hole. Don't program bad shots." *An unvarying routine also is vital*, Miller feels. "Your execution should be the same every time, whether it's for a $2 Nassau or the US Open title. If you change, it fouls up your muscle memory. It's important to have a consistent train of events. The more automatic you become, the more programmed you are, the better you play."

A routine to be followed and has proven to be effective
1. Consistent train of events
    A. believe in every little moment
2. Programmed
3. Automatic

Above all, before you strike the ball, you must be
1.   relaxed
2.   comfortable

There is a definite blending of the senses
1.   Vision
2.   Hearing
3.   Smelling
4.   Taste
5.   Touch

"Our first passageways, he said, are the avenues of sense - our eyes, ears, nostrils, and mouth." Shivas Irons.

"But when I play with my eyes shut, my senses are wide open. My main concern was to see that my general muscular feel and sense of balance went right through to the end." Percy Boomer.

A Full Shot Routine
*   Know your target area—what the architect had in mind when he designed the hole. Play to a level area even if it means longer approach.
*   The yardage to target area—first by sight second by actual paced distance
*   Type of lie—good, bad, flyer, side hill, etc.
*   The shot—how will the elements effect it?
*   Shoot at pin or away from it
*   Where to miss the ball

Mentally visualize the following:
*   The ball's ultimate resting place
*   Trajectory of flight
*   Reaction to the ball upon landing
*   Set up and swing needed for desired shot
*   How the ball feels when it hits the clubface and leaves the clubface—become aware of the sight, sound, and feel of impact

This all takes place before the club is taken out of the bag.

From behind the ball select a spot a few feet out in front of you on the shots starting line (the line is straight and is angled as many degrees left or right of the target as you want to fade or draw the ball).

Set up and align, your feet, hips and especially your shoulders on the imaginary line.

Once you're over the ball your programmed subconscious takes over.

Hogan's Routine

Ben smoked on his cigarette while he weighed the variables of wind, lie, distance, and adrenaline. He was on cruise control now. Because he practiced shots rather than just swings, he had developed an unvarying routine before actually striking the ball: remove the club from the bag definitively, take one last hit from the cigarette and throw it to the ground, eye the target from the side with a little half swing, stand with the club behind the ball and feet together, put the left foot forward then the right foot back, look final time at the target, look back at the ball waggle once, pause hit.

An Inside 90 yards Routine

Before the club comes out of the bag
* type of lie
* the ball's ultimate resting place
* trajectory of flight
* reaction of the ball upon landing
* swing needed for desired shot
* how the ball feels when it hits the clubface

From behind the ball, reaffirm the spot you have selected where you want the ball to land.

A Putting Routine

From a *Golf Digest* article about Bobby Locke . . .

"He had an *unvarying routine* with an old hickory-shafted blade putter. This began with a close examination of the line, even down to what appeared to be a distasteful examination of the hole itself, like a

‌

head waiter examining a bowl of soup which has been the subject of a complaint. People used to joke that Locke reassuring himself that the hole was big enough to receive his ball, but the explanation was less fanciful. Brought up on the nappy greens of South Africa, he had naturally fallen into the habit of inspecting the rim of the cup to confirm the direction of the nap. *And Locke was nothing if not a creature of habit.* After this leisurely reconnaissance he became decidedly brisk. He took his stance, made two quick practice strokes, shuffled an inch or so forward, and hit the putt with a rhythmic, wristy stroke which found the cup in an astonishingly, high proportion of cases.

Q: Payne, could you let us in on the putting routine that's worked so well for you this week?

Payne Stewart: Well, what I did today was I choose the line that I saw the putt, and then once I took my position to the side of the ball, I made two practice strokes with my eyes closed to feel the distance. And then I got up and I aimed my putter on the line that I saw, and I said, "Hold your head still," and I made the stroke. And I didn't do that routine all week long, just today.

Developing a Routine

Possibly the best place to start developing a routine would be on the putting green. Each and every golfer has their own idea about putting and their routine. Pages 89-96 suggest a chapter on putting concepts. This is not to suggest as *the* way to putt, only to illustrate a routine and how and why it takes place. In the moments it takes to read and stroke a putt a lot can happen . . .

Putting Concepts

I. Elementary, my dear Watson

36 fairway shots plus 36 putts = 72.

Seems like half the game. Most know it is more than half the game. When you've got the putter going, your confidence level is soaring. Imagination is the most important factor in good putting.

II. Realize this

"There is nothing more necessary for good putting than to make two entirely separate operations of deciding upon the line and of striking the ball. It is best always to have the first job out of the way so that the entire attention can be given to the second." Bobby Jones.

III. It's a fact, Jack

This author witnessed Jack Nicklaus offer this bit of instruction to his amateur partner, Bob Hoag—who incidentally stayed next to Nicklaus every year for a ten year period (rooms 112 and 114 at the Lodge at Pebble Beach overlooking the 18th green)—during the Crosby. "These are the angles of the putter face (pointing to Hoag's left and right wrists) break your wrists, you move the putter face. Then you'll need a compensating move to square it up again."

IV. Putting is not an exact science

"The putting stroke and the swing with other clubs are basically the same operation." George Low

"My two tenants of good putting, mechanics aside - tempo and practice. These two words will run throughout most everything I say about grip, stance, stoke and so forth. Good putting results from repetition, doing the same thing with the blade every time and a repeating stroke comes from tempo and practice, practice and tempo. That may not sound very precise, but putting is not an exact science—and it does not hurt to understand, that, too." George Low.

"The secret of putting lie in the last two fingers of the left hand." Walter Hagen.

Putting Is a Two-Step Operation
1. Deciding on the line and speed
2. Striking the ball

1. Deciding on the line
"I cannot overstress how vital it is to read every putt accurately before you stroke it." Bobby Locke.

*   First concern is speed—examine from a tripod position the line of the putt to get an overall impression of how hard I should stroke the ball. Give very special attention to the type and length of grass and contours in the immediately vicinity of the hole (4-foot radius). Gradually pull together in my mind a clear picture of the overall pace. Once I have a clear picture of the overall pace. Once I have a clear idea of the pace and how the ball will break around the hole.
*   Return to a position behind the ball and examine the starting line of the putt (makes all putts straight). Major concerns now are the hills and hollows between the ball and the 4-foot radius around the cup.
*   Marry the picture of the ground contour to the picture of the ball running across the green and into the hole.

"Once I have made my mind up about the line and speed I never change it." Bobby Locke.

"After determining the line and speed, I then marrying the two together to form a clear mental image of the putts exact line and speed and falling into the hole." Bobby Locke.

"Even on the smoothest and best kept greens, it is always possible to notice a blade of grass, which will serve as a guide." Willie Park Jr.

"Look for a lighthouse." E. Harvie Ward.

Tips for determining grain direction

Grain grows away from mountains and toward water

If the grass is dull, the grain is running toward you. If the grain is shiny, the grain is running away from you.

Which way would the water run across the green?

Bermuda grass grows toward the setting sun

All putts are straight. The terrain is the break . . . speed determines all putts

"I have holed very few putts where I could not see definitely the path the ball should follow to the hole." Bobby Jones.

Keeping with "the putting stroke and the swing with other clubs is basically the same operation" theory, the actual process of . . .

2. Striking the ball

Getting ready to strike the ball (setup)

"Hold the putter so the blade just touches the grass." George Low.

"Rest the putter lightly on the grass." George Archer.

This author once asked Jack Nicklaus about grip pressure on the putter, and his reply was, "Light but aggressive."

"Hold the club, light, relaxed." Johnnie Miller.

"To avoid movement you must concentrate your weight on the left heel." George Low.

"Your eyes must be directly over the ball." George Low.

"If you expect to take the clubhead back a comfortable distance, allowing your instincts to determine how far, then the chances are pretty good you'll make a slower, rhythmic pass at the ball." George Low.

i. First practice stroke (let's call it a waggle)

"Take a practice stroke at the exact tempo I plan to use for the putt." George Low.

Bobby Locke examined the hole (speed *) and focused on certain parts of the hole or an area around the hole . . .

six inches short of the hole on fast greens

front edge of the hole on medium paced greens

back of the hole on slow paced greens
inside the hole for the short ones

*　　To measure the speed of greens, a ball is rolled off a grooved bar called a stimpmeter. The green is then assigned a rating depending on how many feet the ball rolls. Ratings below 8 are considered slow, while those above 12 are fast.

ii. Second practice stroke (let's call it a waggle)

Incorporate a "feel" into your stroke . . . some ideas:

Left elbow: "The most helpful single thing I was ever able to do to my putting style concerns the left elbow. I was able to create a condition of relaxation and easy freedom I could get in no other way. Although I should, by that time, have learned how deceitful the gods of golf are, I could not resist the temptation to write that this came very close to being a panacea for all putting ailments." Bobby Locke.

Divining rod – Qualified for the 1975 US Amateur using this image. Your arms are the handles and the putter head is the end of the diving rod that never loses its' shape. Webster defines a *divining rod* as a "forked branch or stick alleged to reveal hidden waters or minerals by dipping downward."

Clock's pendulum – "I have always thought of the ideal putter swing as matching that of a clock's pendulum, slow, and very smooth, with the clubhead going through the same distance it goes back. It's a simple repetitive movement and a fine mental picture to have in your mind." Bobby Locke.

The Feel of Impact - what does impact feel like?

Pen logic – One of the tour's better putters is Lauren Roberts. "I think of the shaft as a giant pen." "I'm trying to draw a straight line back with the pen and then a straight line toward my target."

iii. Shuffle forward

"After the rehearsal stroke, you simply slide the club in behind the ball, move your feet forward a tiny bit, then stroke the putt." George Low.

"Continuous but smooth movement is the basis of my putting. Once I have decided how I want to hit the putt, I step up to the ball and do so without ever coming to a complete stop. I take my stance, place the putterhead ahead of the ball, lift it and place it behind the ball then immediately go into the stroke. All this takes a few seconds and keeps me tension free." Julius Boros.

"All I can do is start it and the Lord the takes it from there." Jimmy Demaret.

"Hold my breath and let one go." Walter Hagen.

"Still hog drinks the slop." Lucious Bateman.

After Arnold Palmer won his second Masters title, in 1960, with crucial putts holed on the last two greens, he told the press, "The only thing I did on those two putts was keep thinking what my friend, George Low, always says, 'Keep your head down,'" Al Barkow.

"Staying calm—taking it easy—is the big thing about putting. I try not to worry about the outcome of any putt. That might cause me to move my head when I want it still so as to avoid pushing or pulling the shot." Tony Lema.

"If you become responsive to self 2 (your subconscious) you will know it is ready." W. Timothy Gallwey.

iv. Mental images—blending—becoming one with the ball

"Walter Travis, probably the greatest putter the game has ever seen, always said that he visualized the putting stroke as an attempt to drive an imaginary tack into the back of the ball. I tried the conception and long ago found it to be a valuable aid in putting—to keep in mind the exact line upon which the ball should be started toward the hole. It is all very well to select a point between the ball and hole over which the ball must pass; but is impossible to keep such a point in view, and difficult to keep its location in mind while actually making the stroke. But having selected the spot and allowed the eye to follow the line back to the ball, it is not at all difficult to imagine the line continued through the ball until it emerges at a point on its back side. This is where the tack should be driven—a splendid way of simplifying the operation so that they player can give his entire attention to the making of the stroke." Bobby Jones

In 1976 this author qualified sectionally for the US Open. While playing a practice round at Lake Merced CC (where the regional qualifier was held), playing in front of me was Jerry Barber, the 1961 PGA Champion and the oldest player—at seventy-seven years, ten months, and nine days—ever to play in a PGA tour event (1994 Buick Invitational). Eventually, as play slowed, we caught up with him and his caddy and joined them for a few holes. Quizzed him about his putting technique. He offered this advice, "Ever hammered nails, kid?" Jerry Barber.

"The pictures I want uppermost in my mind is of the line I want the ball to travel on, and how hard I want to hit it." Bobby Jones.

As Jimmy Demaret once noted, chief among Hogan's playing assets was his infinite patience, his willingness to suspend time until he felt completely ready to make the shot required. Until he could properly see the line, in other words, he simply refused to play.

"I've still got the hole in my mind's eye as I putt." Lee Trevino.
Some abstracts to use with your putter:

A lighthouse	Equator
Saucer cup	A tack protruding out of the back of the ball
The putter as a giant pen	

v. Centering

Machines, ledgers, dancers, athletes balance. Just as centering or balance augments various skills, so it may awareness. As an experiment, try standing equally on both feet; then imagine you are shifting your balance slightly from foot to foot: just as balance centers, so do you. If we are conscious in part, this implies more inclusive consciousness. Have you a hand? Yes. That you know without a doubt. But until asked the question were you cognizant of the hand apart?

"As with the golf swing, one should move from center: "We do not feel the clubhead with our hands; we feel it with our bodies . . . this matter of feel at the center is so important that I have coined a name for its seat, for where it is felt. I call it the "force center". I cannot give you an exact anatomical definition of where the force center is, because its position varies with different shots. As the shot (and the swing) become longer, so the force center rises; as they become shorter, the position of the force center drops." Percy Boomer.

"The power is largely produced by the feet and legs, but it is the force-center (somewhere in the pit of your back), which collects it and is responsible for its transfer to the arms and then out to the clubhead." Percy Boomer.

Various Ways to Centering

* Whenever in breath and out breath fuse, at this instant, touch the energyless energy-filled center

* Consider your essence as light rays rising from center up the vertebrae, and so rises livingness in you.

* Place your whole attention in the nerve, delicate as the lotus thread, in the center of your spinal column; in such, be transformed.

* Bathe in the center of sound, as in the continuous sound of a waterfall, or by putting fingers in ears, hear the sound of sounds.

* Imagine the spirit simultaneously within and around you until the entire universe spiritualizes.

* Feel your substance, bones, flesh, blood, saturated with cosmic essence.

* When in worldly activity, keep attentive between the two breaths, and so practicing, in a few days be born anew.

* Abide in some place endlessly spacious, clear of trees, hills, habitations. Thence comes the end of mind pressures.

* At the point of sleep when sleep has not yet come and external wakefulness vanishes, at this point being is revealed.

* Without support for feet or hands, sit only on buttocks. Suddenly, the centering.

* With mouth slightly open, keep in mind the middle of the tongue; or as breath comes silently in, feel the sound HH.

* Simply by looking into the blue sky beyond clouds, the serenity

Moving from center

Lines of energy—from the tail bone up to back of tongue

"I like to feel that my arms and the putter are a one-piece unit; that the putter swings simply because it is an extension of my arms. My arms actually pivot from my shoulders, but I like to feel that a point at the center of the back of my neck is the true pivotal point of the stroke." Bob Charles.

vi. Stroke happens—swing and impact

"If you concentrate solely on the speed you want the putt to travel and hitting the ball squarely on the sweet spot of your putter head - that concentration will automatically produces the length of backswing the putt requires." Sam Snead.

"The key feature is striking the ball with a slightly descending putter - on the downbeat, as I like to say." George Low

Ted Neist, the former head golf professional at Sequoia C. C. in Oakland, who played the tour the same time Bobby Locke played, told me that Bobby used to hit down on all his putts, sometimes taking a small divot on the longer strokes.

Graeme Courts, Loren Roberts's caddie, who sometimes has to remind his boss that his swing wants to go down and through, even with the driver, even with the putter. Especially with the putter. Percy Boomer, a prominent British prewar golf instructor, used to emphasize that one should drive as one putts and vice versa. Roberts says the same thing."

"Shit, man, I thought he was going to cold top some of those putts." Jerry Higgenbotham (Mark O'Meara's caddy when he won the 1998 Master's and British Open) when I asked him if O'Meara hit down or up on his putts.

"Hagen had the answer for my miserable putting when I saw him: 'Just start hitting the ball above the equator,'" Sam Snead.

"Look at the balls original position until the ball vanishes from sight." Bobby Locke.

"Judge 'em by sound." Bobby Locke.

"I don't putt until I'm ready. Any unnecessary movement in a golf swing is disastrous. But in a putting stroke it is a calamity. That's really all I'm doing, waiting and thinking about reducing any unnecessary movement." Ben Hogan.

These hold to be true about putting . . .

"Until all he is conscious of is the feel of the stroke that he will hole the ball." Percy Boomer.

"Firm hitting is the essence of good putting." Bobby Jones.

"The actual striking of the ball is a reflex action caused by proper programming and good concentration." Bobby Locke.

"On some of the greens I would draw my putt into the hole, while others I would cut across the ball and trickle it into the hole." Walter Hagen.

"I could make the ball go in three ways—that is, end over end and by applying spin on it from right to left and from left to right. When you can curl them like that against any break of the green, you have a very fine touch. But it's a young man's touch. It fades in after ten years or so." Sam Snead.

"As I saw it (and still do), Bob Jones was right in 1938 when he said, 'Approximate squareness in striking the ball is all any human can expect to attain. Too much attention to this detail can be very easily overdone. Beyond an approximate square alignment, and added care only causes greater tenseness, which interferes with the fluency of the stroke. And over a sloping green, where touch or pace or range is a factor of importance at least equal to direction, a flowing stroke is a necessity,'" Sam Snead.

"Confidence is 90 percent of putting." Sam Snead.

"One has to be very calm and quiet to putt well. Temperament is preeminently important in putting because good putting is so largely a matter of confidence. You can only stroke the ball when you are quietly confident." Tony Lema.

LOCKE'S SEVEN STEPS TO CONSISTENT PUTTING

1. My left hand grips the shaft of the putter in very much the same fashion as it would any other club, except in this case the left thumb is positioned down the center of the shaft. The grip must be very loose in order to promote a delicate touch. The art of putting lies in the fingers. Feel or touch is so important to me that I have always lengthened the shafts of my putters, as it makes me aware of the weight of the putter head throughout the swing. For the same reason I grip my putter at the very end of the shaft.

2. In placing my right hand on the shaft, I overlap the left in the same way as I do with all other shots, but again the thumb is placed down the center of the shaft. Having my two thumbs pointing straight downward enables me to follow the clubhead through straight in line with the hole and to put topspin on the ball. Topspin is a crucial ingredient to successful putting as it keeps the ball on course.

3. In addressing the ball, I have my weight evenly distributed. I place my feet about four inches apart with the right foot about three inches farther from the line of the putt than my left. In other words, I use a closed stance to prevent myself from cutting across the ball and imparting sidespin. I position the ball directly opposite my left toe, which enables me to strike the ball slightly on the upswing. If the ball were farther back toward my right foot, there may be a tendency to chop or jab it. I actually start with the toe of the putter face behind the ball but eventually strike it with the center of the blade. I find that if you address the ball with the center of the blade, there is a tendency to swing outside the line on the backswing resulting in cutting across the ball during the stroke. Even more important: In addressing the ball near the toe of the putter blade it is easier to take a backswing "inside" the line and to impart topspin at impact.

4. In starting the backswing I make a point of keeping the putter head very low, almost brushing the surface of the green. I make certain that I take the putter back on the "inside." There is no wrist-work at all. Throughout the swing the putter blade must stay square to the hole. While it may be impossible to take other clubs back "inside" without opening their face, it is indeed possible when it comes to putting. My method is based on a technique first introduced by Walter Hagen in the thirties. In keeping the putter square to the hole while taking the club back inside, he talked about "hooding" the face. He proved to me that this is in essence the only backswing with the putter that will consistently apply true topspin. Remember to keep the club head low in the backswing and to eliminate any wrist-work. Watch these points and with practice you will find that it is indeed possible to take the club back "inside" and still keep the blade square to the hole.

5. On completion of the backswing the putter, the left hand and left arm to the elbow are still in one piece. To

These exclusive photographs taken recently for GOLF MAGA-ZINE show that Locke's inimitable style and sartorial taste have remained intact for over 40 years.

make certain that the clubface does not open, the back of my left hand keeps pointing to the grass. I have now in effect reached the "hooding" position and kept the putter face dead square, or if anything, slightly closed. This will ensure true topspin on the ball, provided the putter returns on the same line.

6. At impact the left wrist is still firm in relation to the forearm. The position of the left hand in relation to the putter is exactly the same. This means that the putter blade is being kept square to the hole. Needless to say, my head remains still until the ball has been struck.

7. As I follow through, there is still no wrist work and all the time I am concentrating on keeping the clubface square to the hole and keeping my head down. The follow-through is the same length as the backswing. The putter swing is therefore very much like that of a clock pendulum. Remember: The putting stroke must be slow and smooth and your grip must be loose to promote a delicate and sensitive touch.

Why all this emphasis on topspin? If a ball has true topspin on the green—and the right speed—there are, in fact, three entrances to the hole. There is a front door and there are two side doors. Obviously the safest and surest way is to go for the front door, but with my method, if the ball catches the left side of the hole, or the right, it will drop. True topspin, in fact, gives every one of my putts three chances instead of one.

Mental Aspects

"Competitive golf is played mainly on a five-and-half-inch course. The space between your ears." Bobby Jones.

Sports psychologists or mental skills coaches tailor their teaching to individual golfers, but there are some common themes:

* A sound mental approach can be summed up by what Bob Rotella calls the four Cs: confidence, concentration, composure, and commitment
* Golfers, says Richard Coop, need two types of concentration: disciplined, to consider the factors that go into a shot and execute a pre-shot routine: and flow, that state in which the golfer "lets the swing happen."
* Stay in the present. To play well, golfers have to focus on the shot at hand without dwelling on past shots or worrying about future ones. Put yourself in the best mental state you can for each shot—that's all you owe to yourself
* Aim at specific targets. Instead of thinking about putting your tee shot in the fairway, select a discolored patch of grass. The narrow your focus, the greater margin of error
* Honestly assess your skills. Emphasize your strengths while improving your weaknesses
* Once you're on the course, concentrate on hitting your target. Leave the plethora of mechanical swing thoughts on the practice range while you play

*   Stay within our basic personality style when you play. If it's your nature to smile a lot and chat with others between shots, do it. Having a sound mental game doesn't mean grinding your way around the course without a word for four hours

Flow state—using your right brain. What is your right brain?

The difference between right-brain and left-brain thinking . . .

The left hemisphere is involved with analytical thinking, especially language and logic. Left side of cortex controls right side of the body. Right side of cortex controls left side of the body. The right hemisphere is primarily responsible for our orientation in space, artistic talents, body awareness, and recognition of faces . . . or simply reason vs. passion.

Feeling the right brain

What is the click that tells you that the shot is good before you know it's good . . . maybe that isn't so mysterious? Maybe it's right-brained information that usually gets suppressed by the left brain, but sometimes it gets through before it stops to be translated into words.

And that total concentration is why people take on activities that demand total attention such as mountain climbing, tobogganing, skiing and car racing, where penalties for nonconcentration are so great that even the language using mind shuts up for a minute because it understands that at least for a few minutes, it better get out of the way . . .

The year this author qualified for the US Amateur, it was being played at the James River Course in West Virginia. Playing a practice round with another qualifier who lived and played in the Fort Worth area. His message, "Hogan hit the shot before Hogan hit the shot."

Quotes in support of the right brain thinking concept:

"It is impossible to think without mental pictures." Socrates.

"Where there is conflict between the will and the imagination, the imagination always wins." William James.

"The good golfer, I am convinced, feels where the ball is more than sees it." Percy Boomer.

"The same man who once said he didn't mind mishitting a shot but absolutely detested missing one before he hit it." Ben Hogan, *An American Life*.

"His ability to block out the world's distractions and place himself in a mental state that has replicated the peace and comfort he felt on the practice tee was the final key to unlocking his greatest performances." Ben Hogan, *An American Life*.

"The practice swings of most ordinary players almost always carries most of the main ingredients. The fundamentals are there. But when they are in a match, the difference is terrific. The feet are no longer easily set. There is a cramped body turn. Hands and wrists are rigid. When this happens to me, I began thinking in terms of performance, not results. By this I mean I had no thought beyond the ball—of traps, ponds, rough, or out of bounds. All I did was to go back to my good practice swing, on which I could count, and then to think with my swing—not ahead of the swing." Sam Snead.

"When I swing at a golf ball right, my mind is blank and my body is loose as a goose." Sam Snead.

"I limit myself to just a couple of keys, or conscious thoughts, at any one time in making the swing happen." Sam Snead.

"I don't go into a trance when I address the ball, but maybe I came close to that. I pull the plug out of the part of my brain where the conscious thinking is done, and all the words and thoughts and worries go down the drain. Nothing else exists. My mind is free of facts and fantasies about past, present, and future. If my mind isn't wrapped up in the moment then I'm going to make a mess of it." Sam Snead.

"Look for a lighthouse." E. Harvie Ward.

"Pictures, feelings, and abstracts. The subconscious does not understand English." John Lotz.

"Forget about the left brain activity, and use your right brain when you play golf. Golf is remembered feels." John Lotz.

"How does Picasso paint?" John Lotz.

"Learn to program your computer with pictures, feelings and abstracts rather than instructing yourself with words." John Lotz.

"He told me not only to visualize a shot, but 'audiolize' it—hear the ball hitting the clubface, hear how the divot sounds. This week I wouldn't let myself hit a shot unless I saw it, heard it, and felt it." Notah Begay.

"Learning to see non judgmentally, that is, to see what is happening rather than merely noticing how well or badly it is happening." W. Timothy Gallwey.

"You have to talk to the body in its native language. Its native language is not English, it is sight and feel, mostly sight." W. Timothy Gallwey.

"Visualize. Don't use words. Don't think. Use images. In between shots, count your breath." W. Timothy Gallwey.

"We have to let the body experiment and bypass the mind. The mind acts like a sergeant with the body a private. How can anybody play as a duality?" W. Timothy Gallwey.

"The mind becomes one with what the body is doing, and the subconscious or automatic functions are working without the interference from thoughts." W. Timothy Gallwey.

"'When ye swing, put all yer attention on the feeling o' yer inner body—yer inner body.' He whispered these last words as if he were telling me a secret." Shivas Irons.

"Close yer eyes—feel yer inner body." Shivas Irons.

"Remember the following feeling yer inner body is aye waiting for yer attention." Shivas Irons.

"Put a symbol in the mind and it takes a life of its own." Shivas Irons.

"You can't think and hit at the same time." Yogi Berra.

Golf is a game of constant changes and adjustments. Success in the external game is determined by a player's ability to eliminate psychological barriers, that inhibit the conscious. Only through remembered feels, pictures, and abstracts—a language the subconscious understands—is this possible.

The greatest golfers down the years have recognized that it is impossible to forever "groove" a particular pattern of play, either by ball beating or any other means. Given a basically effective swing, what they've done is continually work on a variety of specific modifications to temporarily achieve a particular desired result, while accepting mentally that the result always will be temporary. The slight modifications will always be temporary.

Many of these modifications occur in the set up. The idea is to understand the fundamentals via left brain and remember them via right brain.

When the left brain interferes . . .

"No matter how clear the complete picture may be, their mind cannot possibly think through the process from beginning to end within the time required for the accomplishment." Bobby Jones.

"Guldahl had also been spectacular despite his funny swing and pace of play that made spectator check their watches. Not only did he win fourteen tournaments during the thirties, but big Ralph won the biggest tournaments. The Western Open was only slightly behind the US Open in prestige when Guldahl won it three times in succession. He also took the US Open in 1937 and 1938 and the Masters in 1939. There was soon a valuable lesson to be gained from Ralph's difficult experiences with sudden fame and wealth. A river of commercial opportunities flooded Guldahl's way, all of which proved mentally distracting to the naturally shy and amiable Texan, among them the lucrative proposition to translate his winning golf touch into an instruction manual. Guldahl, the son of hardworking Norwegians, applied himself diligently to the task of breaking down and explaining the components of his winning golf form. But somehow in the process of trying to explain the physics of his winning unorthodox swing - someone described it as a 'gangly sledgehammer lunge'—Ralph altered the form that carried him to the summit, lost direction, and confidence, and effectively destroying his game." Ben Hogan.

"Pap would tell me in no uncertain terms to permit nobody to fool with my golf swing—and it's a tribute to him that anytime I ever got in trouble with my swing, lost the feel or touch in a shot, it was usually because I became enamored of some popular teacher's ideas about the 'mechanics' of the golf swing and gave the advice a try, often really screwing myself up for a time." Arnold Palmer.

How to eliminate left brain thinking:
In between shots, put your mind on your breathing . . . in, out . . . in, out . . . A quiet mind is the secret of yoga, tennis, golf, soccer goalie, archery, etc.

Playing by feel

"In order to play well, the player must have the feel of the proper stroke. Being unable to view himself objectively, he has no other guide than the sensations produced by the action of his muscles." Bobby Jones.

"By training himself to visualize and plan each shot before he makes it, and by giving careful thought to his method of attack, he can improve his game more certainly than by spending hours on the practice tee." Bobby Jones.

"Walter Hagen found by trial and error, as most of us do, how he could best hit the ball. He had got the feel of his shots, thoroughly into his system and could pull them out whenever he wanted. Long before he plays a shot, the first class golfer has made up his mind how it should feel." Percy Boomer.

"Control through remembered feels." Percy Boomer.

"But when I had developed the idea of control through remembered feeling, I was able to take the word 'think' and 'thought' out of my teaching vocabulary. The results were literally astounding." Percy Boomer.

"Knowledge and thought can never equal muscle memory." Percy Boomer.

"As I've said before, these controls to which feeling a club give the key, are probably muscle memory plus tracks worn in the mind.

But wherever they reside it is clear that the fewer there are of them the more reliable they are likely to be. If I play a pitch one way, a drive another, an iron shot yet another, and a putt quite different again, it is obvious that no single and consistent line of controls will be set up. Confusion as between one set of controls and another is very likely . . . On the other hand if my system is used, a single sound line of controls is set up—by consistently practicing the same fundamental swing for every shot." Percy Boomer.

"These movements are controlled by remembered feel and the only concentrating we must do is guarding this 'remembered feel' from interference." Percy Boomer.

"When you think you have found the secret of some shot that has been evading you—unless what you have 'got' fits into your cycle of sensations or, as we shall now call them, controls. Because unless it does so fit in, it cannot become a reliable part of your game. And why do I call sensations controls? Simple: because I want you to control your golf by these sensations instead of by thought." Percy Boomer.

"The game," as Hogan liked to say, "is all about feel."

"Once your mechanics are reasonably sound "feel" becomes the critical factor and it changes from day to day with one's moods and metabolism." John Lotz.

Develop a feeling storehouse

What is a feeling storehouse? It is a storehouse of key swing thoughts and feels from your best shot making periods. You should consider creating one. The following were entries in my diary over a three-year period . . . this was Mr. Langley's favorite part of the book. Notice the evolvement of left brain thinking to right-brain programming:

Long game
    Feeling of driving my legs to start the downswing

Mental game
    Abstracts instead of specifics

Observation (seeing the difference)
    Playing poorly—programming over ball
    Playing well—programming before club comes out of bag.
    Before shot—gathering abstracts, allowing sensory to work while in motion
    Saw John Enright today. He related a story about when he, Bateman and others attended a tournament and Lucious's observation of an accomplished player . . .   "Looks easy doesn't it? Well, that guy has thought about his grip, his stance, this and that. He just thinks now about hitting the ball. When I was playing good, I had that club out in front of me and I was controlling the club, it wasn't controlling me."

Swing Objectives
    Eliminate foot movement during waggle
    Turn shoulders to 90 degrees
    Breath control
    Balance

Diary Entry
    In practice, work on drawing clear images to execute—that mental aspect of it.
    If you are going to practice, *create the abstracts*.
    Execute your routine with the same mental deliberation you would while playing.
    Make it count. When practicing don't just go through the motions.

***

Diary Entry
    Played well today . . . some concepts in the wheelhouse
    One-pointedness
    Energy streamers
    Here and now
    Right-brain information
    The body's native language is sight and feel—mostly sight
    Breathing exercises
    The right shot at the right moment does not come because you
do not let of yourself

***

Diary Entry
    Short game shuffle—end up with weight on left heel

Diary Entry
    Negative thought patterns, anxiety, depression, fear, etc., put
bad chemicals into your body.
    If you are going to be here . . . why not be positive?
    Life is a school, and you're here to learn lessons
    God loves you

***

Diary Entry
    Composure   Poise   Waggling   Rhythm
    Confidence   Posture   Centering   Timing
    Concentration   Pride   Blending   Balance
    High, low, fade, draw. Breathe deeply. Take time during setup
    What's *centering*? Any six points along the spine . . . they con-
tain certain powers

***

Diary Entry
    Watching ball, maintaining Y, pause, accelerate, hit
    Inverse functioning

Keeping your inner eye on the ball
Left eye to dimple
Mental pictures in the mind's eye
Last two fingers of left hand
Waggle
Rhythm and tone (delay)
Opposition—during movement opposing force in the opposite direction, delaying the clubhead. Feel yourself oppose the weight of the clubhead all the way up, down and through

Diary entry
Played better today. Time in motion or what you have to do in order to achieve the solid hit . . . it is so important to a solid short game.
The feel is the lateral motion of the lower body. What does the finish look like?

***

Diary entry
The sequence—program, capture the lag, allow it to happen

Concentration

"So when a golfer says to me, 'I must learn to concentrate, concentrate, concentrate!' I counter with: "No you must build controls, controls, controls." Percy Boomer.

"When you think you have found the secret of some shot that has been evading you—unless what you have 'got' fits into your cycle of sensations or, as we shall now call them, controls. Because, unless it does so fit in, it cannot become a reliable part of your game. And why do I call sensations controls? Simply because I want you to control your golf by these sensations instead of by thought." Percy Boomer.

'In my mind today the accomplishment of the Grand Slam assumes more importance as an example of the value of *perseverance in the abstract* than as a monument to skill in the playing of the game." Bobby Jones.

"The expert player corrects subconsciously." Bobby Jones.

111

"To remind yourself of six or seven things you "must do" will mess you up. So I take a firm grip on myself and hold my thinking to never more than one idea when I address the ball." Sam Snead.

"Runyan knows how to finish a match better than anybody I've ever seen." Ben Hogan explained to Valerie. "It's his focus. Paul's concentration is so absolute he doesn't seem to see anything but the next shot He wasn't the slightest bit intimidated by my drives. He controlled his mind and mine."

"When I swing at a golf ball right, my mind is blank and my body is as loose as a goose. What I do mean is that, over the past fifty years of playing top-flight competitive golf golf, it seems like my best results have always come when I'm hardly trying at all. At those times my mind and body go on automatic pilot, I swing with my smoothest rhythm and greatest vigor, and the birdie side of each hole opens up for me like I owned the course." Sam Snead.

"The golf swing is a learned motion, an acquired habit. It's damn hard work thinking about what your swing really feels like, and where it could be improved, and what you have to do next to get yourself to play up to your potential." Sam Snead.

Concentration in its purest form is in the here and now. Doing your best at that given moment. Learning from past mistakes and focusing on the here and now—not the future or what has happened.

"If you don't clutter your conscious mind with endless pointers and tips, you make it easier for your subconscious instincts to guide you." Earl Woods.

This profoundly simple notion—Valerie saying to Ben, "Why don't you just hit is closer to the hole?" It gave Hogan an invaluable concrete objective on every shot, a means of staying entirely in the moment instead of getting ahead of himself and fretting about the outcome—an undeniable means of producing more birdies and therefore finally winning. Hogan's path to recovery and breakthrough became "one shot at the time," a credo that not only transformed him in due time, but laid the foundation for the modern performance psychology of the game.

At the time of his success, Dick Lotz (circa 1970) and many of the touring professionals were reading, *Psycho-Cybernetics: A New Way to Get More Living Out of Life* by Maxwell Maltz. While helping Dick move his belongings out of his house from his messy first divorce, this author came across his copy of *Psycho-Cybernetics*, which he, unbelievably, gave to me. Follow in these highlighted passages and some of his own writings that led Dick Lotz (along with some Bateman magic), to the winners circle. This was the mind-set of a champion.

After a short trial, I became convinced that the programming of suggestions into the subconscious mind, utilizing the feedback mechanisms of cybernetics, was the final step that had been needed to make possible the complete reconstruction of the personality as well as changing specific negative habit patterns.

Self-image, the individual's mental and spiritual concept or 'picture' of himself, was the real key to personality and behavior.

Although the science of psychology acknowledged the self-image and its key role in human behavior, psychology's answer to the questions of how self-image exerts its influence, how it *creates* a new personality, what happens inside the human nervous system when the self-image is changed, was "somehow."

The "self-image" is the key to human personality and human behavior. Change the self-image and you change the personality and behavior.

Expand the self-image and you expand the "area of the possible."

Wittingly or unwittingly you developed your self-image by your creative experiencing in the past. You change it by the same method.

"Experiencing" as a direct and controlled method of changing the self-image.

We learn to function successfully by experiencing success.

Experimental and clinical psychologists have proved beyond a shadow of a doubt that the human nervous system cannot tell the difference between an "actual" experience and an experience *imagined vividly and in detail.*

Understanding the psychology of the self can mean the difference between success and failure, love and hate, bitterness and happiness. The discovery of the real self can rescue a crumbling marriage, recreate a faltering career, transform victims of personality failure.

On another plane, discovering your real self means the difference between freedom and the compulsions of conformity.

Each of us carries about with us a mental blueprint or picture of ourselves.

Most of these beliefs about ourselves have unconsciously been formed from our past experiences, our success and failures, our humiliations, our triumphs, and the way other people have reacted to us, especially in early childhood.

In short, you will "act like" the sort of person you conceive yourself to be.

It is literally impossible to really think positively about a particular situation, as long as you hold a negative concept of self.

The new science of "cybernetics" has furnished us with convincing proof that the so-called "subconscious mind" is not a mind at all, but a mechanism—a goal-striving, servo-mechanism consisting of the brain and the nervous system, which is *used by*, and *directed by* the mind. This creative mechanism within you is impersonal. It will work automatically and impersonally to achieve goals of success and happiness, or unhappiness and failure, depending upon the goals which you yourself set for it.

The goals that our own Creative Mechanism seeks to achieve are *mental images*, or mental pictures, which we create by the use of *imagination*. Our creative mechanism works upon information and data which we feed into it.

As you will see later, the method to be used consists of creative mental picturing, creatively experiencing through your imagination, and the formation of new automatic reaction patterns by "acting out" and "acting as if."

The torpedo accomplishes its goal by *going forward, making errors*, and continually correcting them.

Think in terms of the end result, and the means whereby will often take care of themselves.

You must "let it" work rather than "make it" work.

Your nervous system cannot tell the difference between an actual experience and one that is vividly imagined.

Johnny Bulla, the well-known professional golfer, wrote an article several years ago in which he said that having a clear mental image of just where you wanted the ball to go and what you wanted it to do was more important than the "form" in golf. Most of the pros, said Bulla, have one or more serious flaws in their "form." Yet they manage to shoot good golf.

It was Bulla's theory that if you would picture the end —"see" the ball going where you wanted it to go, and have the confidence to "know" that it was going to do what you wanted—your subconscious would take over and direct your muscles correctly. If your grip was wrong, and your stance not in the best form, your subconscious would still take care of that by directing your muscles to do whatever was necessary to compensate for the error in form.

In Dick's own handwriting, he mentioned the following observations.

"At the moment, I have hypnotized myself into a negative attitude about myself."

"Is everyone hypnotized?"

"You can cure your inferiority feelings."

Abstracts

Marvin Leonard made his initial investment in Hogan's second shot at the professional golf winter tour near the end of 1931, allowing Hogan to launch himself out of Cowtown with a grubstake of fifty bucks from Leonard and an additional twenty-five from his brother, Royal. "I left here with $75 in my pocket," he told Ken Venturi in a famous televised interview in 1981. "Would you try that today?" In Phoenix, Hogan won another fifty—his first actual winnings as a professional. By the end of the third week of December, though, he was down to just fifteen cents in his pocket, *forced to eat oranges he picked off the trees* along the fairways of the California courses where he played. He reluctantly wrote his Texas patron asking for another loan. Less than two weeks later, Leonard sent a check for an additional $75 to Los Angeles, where Hogan made zilch. By the time Hogan limped back to the annual Texas Open shindig down in San Antonio in late January of 1932, he was flat broke again, shot 75–80, and withdrew from the tournament.

Put this Equation together . . .

* Bobby Jones, recanting his success in the major championships credited, "the value of *perseverance in the abstract* than as a monument to skill in the playing of the game."

* Shivas Irons: "Put a symbol in your mind and it takes on a life of its own . . ."

* John Lotz: "Concentration in golf is pictures, feelings and abstracts. The subconscious does not understand English."

As John Schlee told me during our lesson—and there's a high probability that Hogan told him the same thing: "Imagine holding an orange between your elbows." Now suppose as Hogan entered the set up phase of his swing visualizing that orange as way to keep his elbows close together—those same oranges he ate to survive during his initial years on tour. Imagine the power in that abstract!

Throughout this book are some abstract that I believe pros use in their thought process . . . now, they may not be these exactly but great players play by pictures, feels, and on a higher level, abstracts. All are individual . . . referenced from this book that apply to the setup and swing:

Percy Boomer—wooden snooker triangle

Sam Snead—the words, thought, worries go down the drain

Ken Venturi—"You open the spring and you close the spring" (visualizing a spring)

Those that apply to putting:

Walter Travis—hitting the tack

Walter Hagen—the equator

Bobby Locke—a clocks pendulum

E. Harvie Ward when assessing the line, Harvey looked for "a lighthouse" (imagine a lighthouse's beam of light)

Jerry Barber—"Ever hammered nails, kid?"

Loren Roberts—"The putter shaft as a giant pen."

In the 2010 NFC Championship the New Orleans Saints won the coin toss in overtime, Brett Favre could only stew on the sideline, wishing for another chance as the Saints drove to the Vikings 22 yard line. Then rookie Garrett Hartley ran out to attempt the winning field goal.

"Just imagine there's a fleur-de-lis between the two goal posts." Sean Peyton, the teams head coach, told Hartley, referring to the team's logo. Hartley's 40-yard kick was perfect.

Lawson Little, Jr.

Lawson Little, Jr. was born in Newport, Rhode Island, and lived much of his early life in the San Francisco area, where his father was a senior military officer at the Presidio of San Francisco. This is where Lawson Jr.'s golf improved explosively. He grew up to be 5' 9" and burly, his 200 pounds so solidly packed that folks started calling him Cannonball. His game had matured even further, despite the fact that Little hardly ever practiced. He had developed a touch around the greens to match his power off the tees. His game struck people first with its power, with his dark, brooding demeanor. his longish wavy hair. . . he looked at all times like an angry senator. The constant traveling that he did as a boy made the younger Little taciturn on his best days and positively prickly on his worst, of which there were considerably more.

By 1930 Little had enrolled at Stanford, and he was making big noise in the world of match play. He became a devoted acolyte of Ernest Jones, the British-born swing coach. Jones's emphasis on a golfer's own instincts for what *felt* (my italics) right in his swing was perfect for a loner like Lawson Little. By 1934 Little was the best match player in the world.

Between 1934 and '35 Little achieved a feat long forgotten by history, but one that was a considerable sensation at the time. He won what was called the Little Slam — winning the U.S. and British Amateurs in consecutive years. This meant he had to win 31 consecutive matches. In 1934, at the British Amateur, the first of these four championships. Wrote Charles Price, "Lawson Little was the greatest matchplayer in the history of golf."

Little occasionally carried 26 clubs in his bag, including seven wedges. (When the USGA adopted the 14-club limit in 1938, it did so largely in response to Little's ever-expanding arsenal.) Answer to the Jeopardy question, "in 1938 his carrying of 26 clubs prompted the USGA to adopt the 14-club limit rule." Who is Lawson Little, Jr?

Little turned pro and immediately signed a number of lucrative endorsement contracts. He never completed the required apprenticeship, so he never became a member of the PGA of America. Nevertheless, he barnstormed the country and won eight professional tournaments, including that 1940 U.S. Open (defeating Gene Sarazen in an 18 hole playoff). With the advent of World War II, Little lost direction as the major championships were cancelled and he became more interested in the stock market than competitive golf. "He never practiced," said Jack Burke Jr. "Little either had it that week or he didn't. But when he did have it, it was lights out."

One of his first sponsors was Wright & Ditson, a sporting-goods company that traced its roots to George Wright, the shortstop of the original Cincinnati Red Stockings. Wright & Ditson eventually sold out to A.G. Spalding's sporting-goods empire, which sold in 1996. Spalding was a massive sporting-goods company with strength in golf, including the Top-Flite and Etonic brands. Eventually the company sold off all its non-golf businesses, renaming the remaining entity Top-Flite. Little was inducted into the World Golf Hall of Fame in 1980.

"I say this without any reservations whatsoever: It is impossible to outplay an opponent you can't outthink." Lawson Little Jr.

"The man who doesn't plan out every shot to the very top of his capacity for thought can't attain championship form," he said. Little also believed, "Winners hit their bad shots best."

Stedman Graham

Stedman was my last caddie gig at the AT&T. At that point in my life, caddying was an opportunity to get behind the ropes to see some great players up close, spend the week with my pals, have some fun and cover expenses. Steady was invited to play in the 1999 AT&T as a guest of Teddy Forstman. Teddy had received nine invitations to the tournament for his charitable contributions to inner-city youth. His foundation, funded with fifty million dollars of his own money, provides educational opportunities for children who demonstrate a passion for education in the middle-school level. These scholarships are for private high school tuition because Teddy believed the public schools in America leave much to be desired. A man of great wealth, yet one with a social conscience, that tells him that providing educational opportunities for the youth of America should be one of our country's top priorities . . . and he puts his money where his mouth is. It is his thought, his heart, and his manner that makes him do things for people . . . especially kids. Imagine if all the millionaires in our country had the same mind-set as Teddy . . . we would be guaranteed a better tomorrow.

Unfortunately, most people only know Stedman as Oprah Winfrey's boyfriend. Obviously (as I learned), he's much deeper, more cerebral than arm candy for Oprah. A native of Whitesboro, New Jersey (founded by his ancestor, former US Congressman George H. White), he is the third of six children and the only one in his family to have completed college. I knew that he was an accomplished basketball player, having played in college, in the US Army in Germany and for a European professional team. He understood the importance of an unvarying routine—all great free-throw shooter have one—but unfortunately, hadn't adopted one into his game. During our practice rounds, I encouraged him to at least apply one to his putting. Like shooting free throws—three dribbles and let one go—if the routine becomes ingrained only your mental state changes the shot. If one could shoot a hundred free throws with the same routine, what would be different if the free throw meant the difference between winning and losing? Only what was in your mind. Because the actual act hasn't changed—the basket isn't any higher, the free-throw line isn't farther away from the basket—only your perception about what's to take place. That's why an unvarying routine is essential for championship golf.

It's no secret that rounds at the AT&T are a six-hour ordeal. There's plenty of time spent standing around. Fortunately, Stedman wasn't put off by my inquisitive mind, and I was able to dig out some of his beliefs and core values. He believes that it does not matter what others may think of you; what matters most is how you feel about yourself, and that, most importantly, you believe in the possibilities in your life. One needs a vision of where you want to go in life. What happens to you is not nearly as important as how you choose to react to it. He spoke of how most people have to deal with some sort of baggage and that you need to learn to see beyond those things and envision a better life. He insisted that there is a process for pursuing success, and *proactive* people do it all the time. Most of those who succeed in achieving their goals do it by creating an *environment for opportunity*. He quoted the philosopher James Allen, "As a man thinketh in his heart, he is." He went on to say that each of us can control our thought process. "There's no telling what you can accomplish when you know who you are and have faith in what you can do."

He stressed, on more than one occasion, that each of us can control our lives by controlling our thought process. "If you can envision a better life for yourself and your loved ones, then you are on the way to creating that life." Talk about right brain thinking!

John Brodie

Quite an athlete, John Brodie. Attended Stanford on a basketball scholarship, quarterbacked the then-Stanford Indians (now the Cardinal) and the NFL football San Francisco 49ers, and played the Senior Tour in its infancy. Could it have been a mind-set that he was able to bring to those different arenas that enabled him to excel in so many sports? A psychologist asked him about the possibility of energy streamers that the golf ball rides to the hole: "Is it possible when a golfer can visualize and execute his shot in a moment of high clarity, could the ball ride the energy streamers right up to the green?"

"I would have to say such things seem to exist. It's happened to me a dozen of times. An intention carries a force, a thought connected with an energy that can stretch itself out in a pass play or a golf shot or a base hit or a thirty-foot jump shot in basketball. I've seen it happen too many times to deny it. The player can't be worrying about the past or the future or the crowd or some other extraneous event. He must be able to respond in the here and now. I believe we all have this naturally; maybe we lose it as we grow up. Sometimes in the heat of the game, a player's perception and coordination improve dramatically. At times, I experience a kind of clarity that I've never seen described in any football story; sometimes it seems to slow way down as if everyone were moving in slow motion. It seems as if I have all the time in the world to watch the receivers run their patterns, and yet I know the defensive line is coming at me just as fast as ever, and yet the whole thing seems like a movie or a dance in slow motion. It's beautiful." John Brodie.

What You Think Is What you Get

The Law of Attraction

The law of attraction is surprisingly simple: like attracts like. It becomes a bit more complicated when it comes to training our minds to think in ways that will bring what we desire into our lives. The term "self-fulfilling prophecy" describes the same law. This well-known term explains that we create the circumstances our mind dwells upon, whether positive or negative. So our goal is to practice consistent presence of mind to make sure our thoughts are always directed toward the positive and that which we want to create.

A key to the process is the word *frequency*. This is true for two reasons: (1) the frequency you use when you passionately dwell upon or revisit a thought, dream, desire or goal provides the energy your musings need for creation and (2) just like a radio station broadcasts on a certain frequency, like the radio you must be "tuned in" to receive it. This means preparing for the arrival of your dream on every possible level—material, physical, and spiritual. You don't have to know how it will come into your life, just trust that it will. Your job is to lay the groundwork, follow any leads you can find, and prepare for its arrival. This can mean cleaning out your garage to make space for a new car, taking a tour of a model home to get the feel of it in order to feed your fantasies, or thinking of what you want in a mate and then living up to that list yourself.

Just like with any skill, the law of attraction must be practiced. We must decide what makes us feel abundant, and use our imagination to create the feeling. It isn't enough to just want something; you must use the power of your thoughts to attract it. A series of choices is what brings us everything in our lives right now, every moment. When we know the direction we want our choices to take us, it is as if we've placed an order with the universe. Then we can await its arrival with joyful anticipation. If we find ways to experience our dreams right now, we make creating joy a treasure hunt in which the seeking is just as much fun as the finding.

Temperament

Anyone whose played golf knows golf is a game of inches. An inch here, you're in bounds, an inch there you've got a swing as opposed to a restricted swing. Some lose their minds cursing their luck while the knowledgeable player realizes staying in the moment – no matter the outcome of any shot – is the key to long term success. Some think of it as non judgemental awareness. Place no value on the birdies, bogeys, bad breaks and continue on. Mindfulness means paying attention to what's happening in the present moment without interpretation or judgement in the now. Play the long game. You don't have to be the chosen one. If you're patient, the plateaus will become springboards.

"If you wish to hide your character, do not play golf. It will be revealed on the golf course. I was telling this one day to a very irascible chap, and he said, 'Well what would you do about it, if you were me?' I replied quietly, 'Ride a bicycle,'" Percy Boomer.

"I suppose everyone would agree that 'self-control' as effective as that possessed by men like Hagen and Harry Vardon is a priceless quality. But how to achieve it? It can only be done by building one's golf into a closed, self-controlling circle, and then keeping extraneous matters outside that circle." Percy Boomer.

Is there a psychology for winning? I don't understand the psychological function of the human mind sufficiently to answer that very well, except to say that winners are different. They're a different breed of cat. I think the reason is, they have an inner drive and are willing to give of themselves whatever it takes to win. It's a discipline that a lot of people are not willing to impose on themselves. It takes a lot of energy, a different way of thinking." Byron Nelson.

"An old-timer in Scotland once said to me, 'Make your game as storm proof as you can,'" Sam Snead.

"The lesson you never want to forget is that you can't stay mad in golf without it hurting you." Sam Snead.

"The right idea of course, is not only never lose your temper while you are playing golf, but not ever to feel like losing it. This is an impossible goal to achieve, but the nearer a golfer can get to it the more effective a player he will be." Tony Lema.

"A great many of them like Palmer, were taught the game by a father who was a golf professional. Also, as I pointed out earlier, college golf has really blossomed as the training ground for the pro tour. These players knew when they joined the tour what it has taken me five years on the tour to learn: how to maintain consistency, to play the difficult shots that suddenly bob up at critical moments, to keep emotional control under pressure." Tony Lema.

"Playing golf is 30 percent physical and 70 percent mental. Lose control of the mental side and you were only 30 percent a golfer." Tony Lema.

"The most important thing to keep, in golf, is a good attitude and a clear mind." Tony Lema.

"I never pray on the golf course. Actually, the Lord answers my prayers everywhere except on the golf course." Billy Graham.

"Never break your putter and driver in the same round or your dead." Tommy Bolt.

"If you are going to throw a club, it is important to throw it ahead of you, down the fairway, so you don't have to waste energy going back to pick it up." Tommy Bolt.

After losing the 1996 Masters to Nick Faldo, Greg Norman, returned to Augusta for the 1997 Masters. "The way they treated me in the locker room, in the clubhouse, the way the fans responded to me, it was all different." The loss in 1996, and his return a year later, "helped me understand the meaning of the game," he said. "That is, in golf, how you handle yourself is more important than what you shoot. There are certain moments in your life that change you. You can fight them or embrace them but you'd be an idiot not to embrace them."

Golf is 20 percent mechanics and technique, the other 80 percent is philosophy, humor, tragedy, romance, melodrama, companionship, camaraderie, cussedness, and concentration.

"Baseball is 90 percent mental. The other half is physical."
Yogi Berra.

Tom Morris

Tom Morris designed over 60 courses. Each course he laid out
was "the finest in the kingdom, second only to St. Andrews"... at
least until he laid out the next one. Tom showed novice greenskeep-
ers how to top dress and rake putting greens. He pioneered inland
golf by introducing horse drawn mowers for fairways and push mowers for greens. In 1886 Tom went to Dornoch, in the Highlands 110
miles north of St. Andrews to extend the links there to 18 holes. The
Dornoch Golf Club's junior champion was a boy named Donald
Ross. Five years later Ross left home to work for Tom at St. Andrews.
Ross returned to Dornoch for a stint as the club's greens-keeper
before moving to America in 1899. Over the next half century he
would design Pinehurst #2, Seminole, Oak Hill, Oakland Hills and
400 other courses. Even if Tom Morris had never seen Prestwick or
planted a flag at County Down, his influence on Ross would still
make him a critical figure in the game's evolution. But Ross was only
one of his disciples. Charles Blair McDonald kept a locker in Tom's
shop before he crossed the Atlantic to build America's first 18 hole
course at the Chicago Golf Club and won the first U.S. Amateur
Championship. Alistar MacKenzie studied Tom's handiwork.
MacKenzie titled his book on course design *The Spirit of St. Andrews.*
Albert Tllinghast, who learned the game from Tom, went on to lay
out Baltusrol, Bethpage, San Francisco Golf Club and Winged foot.
Tom Morris chief contribution to the game may have been in course
design, a multibillion-dollar business that grew from the barrow,
spade and shovel he used at Prestwick and St. Andrews.

Tom kept his chin aimed toward heaven. Being gloomy was
a bit of a sin, he said, because it suggested that we know the Lord's
business better than He does. In the fall of 1895 Tom played in his
last British Open. He was seventy-four years old. He had played in
twenty-seven Open Championships, including the first fourteen,
winning four times. His competition were small beer compared to
the one who must never be forgotten. "I could cope with 'em all"

on the course, said Tom. "All but Tommy. He was the best the old game ever saw." Just inside the R & A clubhouse is a glass display case that holds the Claret Jug. The first name on the trophy is TOM MORRIS JNR. The Claret Jug may be the most important trophy in golf, but it is not alone in its display case. Above it hangs another prize: Tommy's Championship Belt.

Walter Hagen

There is some debate among golf historians as to whether Hagen should actually be credited with 16 major championships, second only to Jack Nicklaus and two ahead of Tiger Woods. (However, counting the U.S. Amateur, which is no longer considered a major championship, Woods's three Amateurs titles gives him a total of 17, three behind Nicklaus's 20.) Hagen captured the Western Open five times (1916, '21, '26, '27, and '32), at a time when the Western Open was considered one of the premier events on the world golf schedule, second only to the U.S. and British Opens. In Hagen's prime, the Masters had not yet been founded, and the Western Open (the championship of the Western Golf Association) was, by today's definition, a "major", insofar as it was one of four elite tournaments in which most of the top golfers in the world could be counted on to participate each year.

"All the professionals . . . should say a silent thanks to Walter Hagen each time they stretch a check between their fingers. It was Walter who made professional golf what it is." Gene Sarazen.

The touring pros of today should take a course in golf tour history—the touring professionals. Those who paved the way for their fifteen minutes of fame. Hagen was the man. He was the first full-time, unattached touring professional. After winning the 1919 US Open, he resigned his post at Oakland Hills Country Club for a life of tournaments, exhibitions, and drinking champagne from women's spike-heeled shoes. Certainly Bobby Jones, Byron Nelson, Ben Hogan, Sam Snead, Arnold Palmer, Jack Nicklaus, Tiger Woods, and countless others merit consideration, but Hagen did more for the game—he brought it to the world.

At his peak during the 1920s, Sir Walter raked in more than $300,000 a year from tournament winnings and lucrative exhibitions matches, a fortune in the world of professional sports and as much as any athlete in the world made at the time. "I never wanted to be a millionaire," he confided on the cover of his best-selling autobiography. "I just wanted to live like one."

In 1930s, traveling by boat to Japan (later toured by Bill Melhorn and Bobby Cruicshank) and Australia with his traveling companion the trick shot artist, Joe Kirkwood. The great champion staged many exhibitions . . . worldwide. During this period, golf professionals were considered to be second-class citizens. Their primary duty was to serve the membership. They could only enter the clubhouse through the service entrance. The golf tour at that time was played by nomadic club pros over the winter between their club's closing day and springtime opening day. Those in the know realize he single-handedly brought the club pro out of the "pro shop and into the clubhouse." These quotes seem to give an insight to the persona he tried to create, his diplomacy and mental approach to competing, to being a champion . . .

"I learned early that whatever I got out of life, I'd have to go out and get for myself. And the physical aptitude I possessed gave me the means of beginning. However, I had to create a paying market for that ability to play golf. Showmanship was needed and happily I possessed a flair for that too and I used it. In fact, some fellows believed I invented the kind of showmanship which began to put golf on a big time money basis. Apparently, too, it pleased the public to think I lived the easy carefree life, the playboy of golf. Frankly I was happy to support both those illusions, since I was making money out of the showmanship and I was having a grand time living on the money. I was trying to make a living out of a game which had never in its history supplied more than the bare necessities to its professional players." Walter Hagen

Some of Hagen's pearls of wisdom. . . .

Mode of Action

* Saving time and spending it properly.
* People care about their own worries, not about mine.
* Looked and acted the role of a champion.
* Hit or miss, make your deadpan expression never change.
* A touch of nobility as if looking into the setting sun.
* How a real professional golfer must dress.
* I usually arrived with just enough time to swing a club before teeing off

Mental Approach

* Concentrate on playing the best you can each shot . . . if it's a good one, that's fine. If it's bad, forget it. I expect to make so many bad ones anyway.
* I realized long ago that I'm no machine. I'm just human like the next fellow. And I'm going to make plenty of shots that will make me look like the rankest beginner. But if I let a blunder like that get to me, I'd have kicked away every championship or challenge match I'd ever played. I had to recognize that fact and aim to get the good ones where it counted most.
* Keen, fresh, eager, when play started.
* Look at each round as a unit and take individual bad shots in my stride.
* The fellow who can give himself a quick shake and release the physical tension can go on to play championship golf.
* The most important quality in my mental approach to golf competition was the fact I could forget the last bad shot and concentrate on the next.
* For no one knew better than I the value of relaxation.
* I would stride erect down the fairway.
* I'd become acclimated to the day and the conditions.
* I never hurry. From the minute I rose in the morning I kept on an even keel until I reached the first tee. There's a certain sort of rhythm in such a routine that carried over into my game.

* Never hurry, never worry and always remember to smell the flowers along the way.
* I could make a highball last longer in my own glass than any Scotchman ever born.
* The sun don't shine on the same dog's tail all the time.
* I could take a beating and still smile.

From the author's perspective, every shot, he pretended to be racked with doubts. He'd study his lie, he'd walk ahead to survey the green, finger his clubs with uncertainty, he'd shake his head, address the ball and back away to change clubs.

* I always used a lot of strategy and psychology. I used it on them all. I set up shots the way a movie director sets up scenes . . . To pull all the suspense possible from every move. I strutted and smiled.
* Accept the highs and lows.
* Tell both the pluses and the minus sides. Take the total and let it stand.
* When a tournament is over—forget it.
* Luck . . . sometimes we have it, sometimes we don't

Personal favorite Hagen story . . . Hagen, the reigning PGA Champion. sailed to Great Britain a few weeks before the 1928 British Open to play an exhibition match with the best European player at the time, Archie Compston. Their 36-hole exhibition match lasted until the 19th hole, whereupon Hagen graciously smiled, shook the big fellas hand and offered his congratulations. Upon entering his awaiting limousine, he announced to the driver, "I could beat that son of a bitch any day of the week." Which he did two weeks later in the British Open, outdistancing the third place finisher, Archie Compston by two shots. Among the many pictures in his book are two, one of Hagen shaking Archie Compston's hand after their exhibition and the other at the awards ceremony for the British Open. Hagen's expression is nearly identical in both pictures! The tournament's first prize, only L75. Hagen consider the sum so insignificant that he gave all of it to his caddy. The voyage back to New York was filled with merriment, a time for reflection, and living large. Borrowing whatever money his son had for gratuities, Hagen had his agent book the top floor of the Waldorf Astoria, casually mentioning that he needed a few exhibitions to pay for the rooms.

Hagen captained the United States in the first six Ryder Cups, and played on the first five U.S. teams: 1927, 1929, 1931, 1933, and 1935. Hagen became the first professional golfer to open a golf equipment company under his own name. Hagen was inducted into the World Golf Hall of Fame, in the charter class of 1974.

"When the Haig died . . . in 1969, Junior called me from Detroit to tell me there would be no funeral. Instead, a bunch of his cronies were going to throw a party at the Detroit Athletic Club. They thought the Haig would prefer that. I didn't go. Like Hamlet, golf's sweet prince, I thought deserved a grander exit than that. He was splendid. They should have carried him out on a shield." Charles Price.

Walter Hagen

Bobby Jones

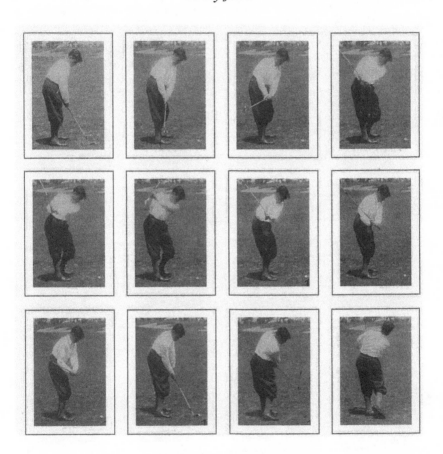

Gene Sarazen

Ben Hogan

Photos by Chuck Brenkus

Byron Nelson

Photos by Chuck Brenkus

Sam Snead

Jack Nicklaus

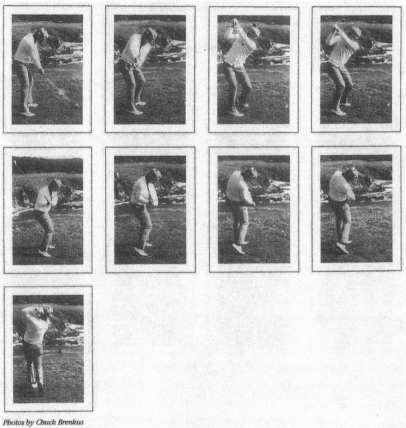

Photos by Chuck Brenkus

Miller Barber

Celebrity Sweepstakes

"We were very anxious and pleased to have people like Bob Hope and Sammy Davis and Dean Martin ... all the guys who were celebrities who put their names on golf tournaments," Arnold Palmer said. "It helped in a couple of ways. It helped with the general public and got attention to the tournament itself. It also encouraged amateurs to participate in the pro-am and to come and be a part of the tournament. And it did help with corporate sponsors, too. It was very important to the game and the professional tour."

The Crosby & The Hope became synonymous with tour stops in Pebble Beach & Palm Springs, respectively. San Diego had Andy Williams. Los Angeles had Glen Campbell. Danny Thomas had Memphis, Tennessee, Dinah Shore had Palm Springs. Fort Lauderdale belonged to Jackie Gleason, Dean Martin had Tucson, & Sammy Davis Jr had Hartford, Connecticut.

Bing Crosby 1937-1985

The first multimedia star, Crosby was a leader in record sales, radio ratings, and motion picture grosses from 1931 to 1954. His early career coincided with recording innovations such as the microphone. This allowed him to develop an intimate singing style that influenced many male singers who followed him, including Frank Sinatra and Dean Martin. According to *Guinness World Records*, Irving Berlin's song "White Christmas", sung by Bing Crosby with the Ken Darby Singers, remains the best selling single of all time. It has sold over 100 million copies around the world, with at least 50 million sales as a single. His recording was so popular that he was obliged to re-record it in 1947 using the same musicians and backup singers as the original 1942 master.

Crosby first took up the game at 12 as a caddy, dropped it and started again in 1930 with some fellow cast members in Hollywood during the filming of "The King of Jazz." Although he made his name as a singer, vaudeville performer and silver screen luminary, he would probably prefer to be remembered as a two handicap who competed in both the British and U.S. Amateur championships, a five-time club champion at Lakeside Golf Club in Hollywood, and as one of only a few players to have made a hole-in-one on the 16th at Cypress Point.

He was elected to the World Golf Hall of Fame in 1978.

Founded in 1937, the **Bing Crosby National Pro-Amateur** hosted the first National Pro-Am Golf Championship in southern California at Rancho Santa Fe Golf Club in San Diego County, the event's location prior to World War II. Sam Snead won the first tournament, then just 18 holes, with a winner's share of $500. A second round was added in 1938 and was played through 1942. After the war, it resumed in 1947 as a 54-hole event, up the coast on golf courses near Monterey, where it has been played ever since. In 1947 of that year, the tourney was played at Pebble Beach Golf Links, Cypress Point Club, and Monterey Peninsula Country Club. The tournament became a 72-hole event in 1958. The event was originally known as the Bing Crosby **National Pro-Amateur**, or just the **Crosby Clambake**. After the 1985 event The Crosby name was dropped and AT&T Corporation became the title sponsor in 1986. It is organized by the Monterey Peninsula Foundation.

Celebrity Golf 1961-1962

Pro Sam Snead tees it up for nine holes with celebrity challengers in this 1961-1962 television series with a thousand dollars going to cancer research in the name of the winner. It featured a who's who of Hollywood – Bob Hope, Milton Bearle, Mickey Rooney, Jerry Lewis, Harpo Marx, Perry Como, Dean Martin, Danny Thomas, Randolph Scott and 17 other noted celebrities. Each episode is hosted by Harry Von Zell and filmed at Lakeside Country Club. At the end of each match, Snead gives the celebrity golfer a lesson in the finer points of the game.

Frank Sinatra – 1963

An American singer, actor, and producer who was one of the most popular and influential musical artists of the 20th century. He is one of the best-selling music artists of all time, having sold more than 150 million records worldwide.

In July of 1953, Sinatra made an overseas trip to Scotland. Battling a career slump – he had scheduled a series of concerts in Glasgow, Ayr and Dundee – the trip came at a particularly crucial time. While in Scotland, Sinatra found time to attend The Open Championship in Carnoustie. He wanted to support Ben Hogan, who was making his first – and only – start at The Open Championship. Hogan had won the first two majors that season and Sinatra, having been bitten by the golf bug, was curious to see if Hogan could win the third leg. Sinatra was on hand Thursday morning to see Hogan shoot 71 in the second round (the last two rounds were played on Friday) and declared that "all America is rooting for Hogan."

Three months later, the movie "From Here to Eternity" was released. It would win eight Oscars, including Sinatra as best supporting actor. Sinatra's admiration for Hogan never wavered. According to Golf Digest, Sinatra once hired Hogan to be the teaching pro at his club in Palm Springs.

Just a few years after Bing Crosby started up his namesake tournament at Pebble Beach – and before Bob Hope or Andy Williams added their names to other tournaments in California – Sinatra hosted his own TOUR-sanctioned event, the **Frank Sinatra Open Invitational**, in November of 1963 at the Canyon Club in Palm Springs. Sinatra was a resident, and his Rat Pack crew as well as other celebrities usually holed up at the club.

It was played for only a single year—1963—although it was intended to be an annual affair. The five-day event was designed for the mixture of touring pros and celebs to fit the party lifestyle, with a black-tie affair at the Palm Springs Riviera Hotel following the four days of competition. It allowed the heavyweights in golf and show business to come together and pay tribute to the icon who meant so much to both industries.

First place prize money was $9,000, which was in the upper echelon for winner's earnings in 1963. Two years later, Hope officially became the namesake of the Desert Classic and the birth of one of the biggest celebrity events on TOUR was complete.

During that 1963 tournament, 150 deep-pocketed amateur players were given a custom-made putter designed by Sinatra's good friend, former TOUR pro and noted golf-club maker Toney Penna. Sinatra originally wanted the putter made of solid gold, but Penna told him the club would be too heavy and unusable. Instead, Penna – using the shape of a popular Tommy Armour putter – used forged steel and copper-plating. The MacGregor IMG-5 heel-shafted putter had Sinatra's signature and a small caricature of his likeness engraved on the club sole.

Bob Hope 1965-2011

An English-American stand-up comedian, vaudevillian, actor, singer, dancer, athlete, and author. With a career that spanned nearly 80 years, Hope appeared in more than 70 short and feature films, with 54 feature films with Hope as star, including a series of seven "Road" musical comedy movies with Bing Crosby as Hope's top-billed partner. In addition to hosting the Academy Awards show 19 times, more than any other host, he appeared in many stage productions and television roles, and was the author of 14 books. The song "Thanks for the Memory" was his signature tune.

He was praised for his comedic timing, specializing in one-liners and rapid-fire delivery of jokes which often were self-deprecating. He is often credited with having helped create the modern American version of stand-up comedy. Celebrated for his long career performing in United Service Organizations (USO) shows to entertain active duty American military personnel, making 57 tours for the USO between 1941 and 1991, Hope was declared an honorary veteran of the U.S. Armed Forces in 1997 by an act of the United States Congress. He also appeared in numerous specials for NBC television starting in 1950, and was one of the first users of cue cards.

Since the 1920s he has been one of the sport's great ambassadors. As he traversed the globe entertaining both black-tie audiences and battalions of scruffy soldiers. He teamed with Arnold Palmer to win the pro-am portion of the Palm Springs Desert Classic in 1962. Three years later Hope took the reigns of that tournament, which donned his name – the Bob Hope Classic – from 1965 to 2011. He was elected to the World Golf Hall of Fame in 1983.

Originally known as The Palm Springs Golf Classic, it was changed in 1965 to **The Bob Hope Desert Classic**, then in 1984 to **The Bob Hope Classic**, then in 1986 to **The Bob Hope Chrysler Classic**, then in 2009 – 2011 to **The Bob Hope Classic,** from 2012 to 2015 it became The Humana Challenge. In 2016 it became The CareerBuilder Challenge. It is a professional golf tournament in southern California on the PGA Tour. Played in mid-winter in the Coachella Valley(greater Palm Springs), it is part of the tour's early season "West Coast Swing." Known for its celebrity pro-am, it previously had five rounds and four different courses – 90 holes 0f competition rather than the standard 72 holes of four rounds. (In 2012, the Humana changed to a traditional 72-hole format over three different courses with a 54-hole cut, similar to the AT&T Pebble Beach Pro-Am). "The Hope" is organized by the nonprofit Desert Classic Charities.

Andy Williams 1968-1988

An American singer, he hosted The Andy Williams Show, a television variety show, from 1962 to 1971, and numerous TV specials. The Andy Williams Show won three Emmy awards. The Moon River Theatre in Branson, Missouri is named after the song for which he is best known —Johnny Mercer and Henry Mancini's "Moon River". It has sold more than 100 million records worldwide, including more than 10 million certified units in the United States

The San Diego Open was founded in 1952 but hop-scotched around southern California for its first 16 years, never really finding a home. Back in 1968, Williams came aboard and agreed to become the celebrity host of the San Diego Open Invitational on the PGA Tour – this was the golden era of celebrity golf events. Williams was an avid golfer, and frequently played in the pro-am portion of the Crosby and the Hope celebrity-filled events.

That same year that the tournament moved to Torrey Pines, and the combination of celebrity clout and first-class venue proved to be a real game-changer. The event has remained at Torrey ever since and become one of the most successful on the PGA Tour – and no doubt that success helped to pave the way for Torrey to be awarded the 2008 U.S. Open, won by Tiger Woods in his memorable 18-hole playoff over Rocco Mediate.

Williams served as celebrity host of the San Diego Open for 21 years –

1968-1980 **Andy Williams-San Diego Open Invitational 1968-1980**

1981-1982 **Wickes-Andy Williams San Diego Open**

1983-1985 **Isuzu-Andy Williams San Diego Open**

1986-1987 **Shearson Lehman Brothers Andy Williams Open**

1988 **Shearson Lehman Hutton Andy Williams Open**

only the Hope and Crosby affiliations with their events lasted longer. Williams eventually shared title billing with sponsors like Isuzu and Shearson Lehman Brothers, and his name finally disappeared from the title in 1989. The tournament is now known as the Farmers Insurance Open.

Danny Thomas 1970-1984

One of 10 children, Thomas was an American nightclub comedian, singer, actor, and producer whose career spanned five decades. He began his career perfoming on the radio in Detroit WMBC on The Happy Hour Club in 1932. Thomas first performed under his anglicized birth name, "Amos Jacobs Kairouz." After he moved to Chicago in 1940, he changed his name to "Danny Thomas" (after his two brothers). He created and starred in one of the most successful and long-running situation comedies in the history of American network television, in addition to guest roles on many of the comedy, talk, and musical variety programs of his time.

In his time of hopelessness and despair, he turned to the church. Praying to St. Jude Thaddeus, the patron saint of hopeless causes, Danny asked the saint to "help me find my way in life, and I will build you a shrine." In the years that followed, Danny's career flourished through films and television, and he became an internationally known entertainer. He remembered his pledge to build a shrine to St. Jude.

In the early 1950s, Danny began discussing with friends what concrete form his vow might take. Gradually, the idea of a children's hospital, possibly in Memphis, Tennessee, took shape. In 1955, Danny Thomas and a group of Memphis businessmen who had agreed to help support his dream seized on the idea of creating a unique research hospital devoted to curing catastrophic diseases in children. More than just a treatment facility, this would be a research center for the children of the world.

Danny felt that "no child should die in the dawn of life," so he declared a personal war against the killer diseases that strike the young. He started funding the hospital in Memphis in 1957. Great names in medicine led the research. Plenty of impossible things were made possible because Danny stuck to his mission like a bulldog. In 1962, only 4 percent of the victims of acute lymphocytic leukemia survived the disease; in 1991, 73 percent survived. Only 7 percent of patients with nonHodgkin lymphoma recovered; now, about 80 percent do. The list goes on and on. When people tell you about the "impossible," just think of St. Jude's Hospital.

In 1969, he agreed to lend his name to the tournament in exchange for his St. Jude Children's Research Hospital becoming the tournament's charity. Accordingly, the tournament changed its name the next year to the Danny Thomas Memphis Classic where the title remained until 1984. In 1977, President Gerald Ford, who had left office in January, made a hole-in-one during the tournament's celebrity pro-am while playing with Thomas and Ben Crenshaw. Two days later, Al Geiberger shot a PGA Tour record 59 (–13) in the second round with eleven birdies and an eagle.

1958-1959	Memphis Open
1960-1969	Memphis Open Invitational 1960-1969
1970-1984	**Danny Thomas Memphis Classic**
1985	St. Jude Memphis Classic
1986–1994	Federal Express St. Jude Classic

1995-2006	FedEx St. Jude Classic
2007-2008	Stanford St. Jude Championship
2009	St. Jude Classic presented by FedEx
2010	St. Jude Classic presented by Smith & Nephew
2011-now	FedEx St. Jude Classic

Although it no longer bears Thomas' name, the tournament continues to support the St. Jude Children's Research Hospital.

"Success in life has nothing to do with what you gain in life or accomplish for yourself. It's what you do for others." Danny Thomas

Glen Campbell 1971-1983

An American singer, guitarist, songwriter, television host, and actor. He was best known for a series of hit songs in the 1960s and 1970s. He began his professional career as a studio musician in Los Angeles, spending several years playing with the group of instrumentalists later known as "The Wrecking Crew". After becoming a solo artist, he placed a total of 80 different songs on either the *Billboard* Country Chart, *Billboard* Hot 100, or Adult Contemporary Chart, of which 29 made the top 10 and of which nine reached number one on at least one of those charts. He released over 70 albums in a career that spanned five decades, selling over 45 million records worldwide. He hosted a music and comedy variety show called The Glen Campbell Goodtime Hour on CBS television, from January 1969 until June 1972. Campbell played a supporting role in the only film John Wayne won an Oscar, *True Grit* (1969).

"Golfers were a fraternity he liked, maybe even more than entertainment people," Eddie Merrins, the renowned professional (now professional emeritus) at Bel-Air Country Club, wrote in his book, Playing A Round with the Little Pro: A Life in Golf. "He loved to play in the Crosby. When he played, he played to win. As a musician he succeeded because of work and love of the business. He had the same attitude about golf."

His greatest contribution to the game was lending his name to the Los Angeles Open – one of the longest running tour events - at a time it was floundering. The Junior Chamber of Commerce that ran the tournament at the time was lagging behind other tournaments in prize money, notably its competition to the south, the Andy Williams San Diego Open Invitational. In 1970, the year before Campbell came aboard, the Los Angeles Open had a purse of $100,000, or $50,000 less than San Diego was offering. Moreover, it was being played at the municipal Rancho Park Golf Course.

Meanwhile, his television show, the Glen Campbell Goodtime Hour, aired on CBS as did the Los Angeles Open. The Junior Chamber of Commerce, CBS and Campbell got together and the Glen Campbell Los Angeles Open debuted in 1971. By 1973, it had moved to the Riviera Country Club, where it remains today, and by 1976 the purse had risen to $185,000, exceeding San Diego's purse. The tournament history:

1926-1970	Los Angeles Open
1971-1983	**The Glen Campbell Los Angeles Open**
1984-1986	Los Angeles Open
1987-1988	Los Angeles Open by Nissan
1989-1994	Nissan Los Angeles Open
1995-2007	Nissan Open
2008-2016	Northern Trust Open
2017-2018	Genesis Open

Campbell, meanwhile, joined Bel-Air Country Club and took lessons from Merrins.

"Glen loved to play the game and, at one time, was a legitimate 3-handicap player," Merrins wrote. "He was forever picking my brain for things that would help him make a better swing. I don't think I've ever been around him when we didn't talk about the golf swing or a piece of equipment."

Dinah Shore 1972-1999

Born Frances Rose Shore in Winchester, Tennessee in 1916. Like Elvis, she began her singing career in Memphis. She gained fame on the radio in the late 1930s in duets with Frank Sinatra and later on Eddie Cantor's show. She was one of America's first television stars, first on "The Chevy Show," which ran from 1951 to 1961, and later on the Dinah Shore Show, "Dinah's Place," and "Dinah!" She won 10 Emmy Awards, nine gold records and a Peabody Award.

Shore, who didn't take up golf until age 52, was a longtime supporter of women's professional golf. Once Shore fell for the game, she fell hard. She became the first female member at Los Angeles' tony Hillcrest Country Club, and her home away from home was Mission Hills in Rancho Mirage, where she had a house off the ninth green. She became the first woman to play in PGA TOUR pro-ams at San Diego and Westchester. She was the first female member of Hillcrest Country Club.

In 1972 along with Colgate-Palmolive chairman David Foster, she helped found the Colgate Dinah Shore Golf Tournament. Its debut was a 54 hole event and was the richest event in women's golf; its purse was more than double that of the LPGA Champion-ship or the U.S. Women's Open. The first edition invited all winners of tour events from the previous ten seasons. Shore's name helped insure network television coverage back when it was a precious commodity, which in turn helped her tournament set the curve for purse increases. Since its inception, it has been held annually at the Mission Hills Country Club in Rancho Mirage, California, southeast of Palm Springs. The tournament has been classified as a major since 1983.

1972–1980	**Colgate-Dinah Shore Winner's Circle**
1981	**Colgate-Dinah Shore**
1982	**Nabisco Dinah Shore Invitational**
1983–1999	**Nabisco Dinah Shore**
2000–2001	Nabisco Championship
2002–2014	Kraft Nabisco Championship
2015–present	ANA Inspiration

It is the first major of the year, usually played in late March or early April. In acknowledgment of her contributions to golf, Shore was elected posthumously an honorary member of the LPGA Hall of Fame in 1994. Shore became a member of the World Golf Hall of Fame when it absorbed the LPGA Hall in 1998. She received the 1993 Old Tom Morris Award from the Golf Course Superintendents Association of America, GCSAA's highest honor.

The ANA Inspiration remains one of the major golf tournaments on the LPGA Tour. The tournament is held each spring at Mission Hills Country Club, near Shore's former home in Rancho Mirage, California. For all the good times her tournament generated, Shore's legacy is steeped in far more important matters. "I don't like discrimination on the basis of sex," the First Lady of Golf once said. "Ability is the only thing that matters. The tournament we play is awfully powerful proof of that."

Jackie Gleason 1972-1980

Gleason was 45 and a show-business legend. Christened "The Great One" by Orson Welles after a long and liquid night on the town, Jackie Gleason embraced all that the title implied. A novice to golf—in the Brooklyn neighborhood where he was raised the games were turnstile jumping and hustling pool—Gleason had hosted one of the most successful TV variety shows in the 1950s, and during one magical year in 1956 filmed all 39 episodes of The Honeymooners. These were the early days of television, before UHF, cable, DVDs and DVRs, and The Jackie Gleason Show averaged a Nielsen rating of 42.4 for the 1954-55 season, which meant that 42.4 percent of the nation's households with television sets were tuned to Gleason's show. For perspective, the 2009 Super Bowl received a 42.0 Nielsen rating.

During that Honeymooners season, Gleason was learning to play golf, which led to the classic "Ralph Learns to Play Golf" episode, where Gleason's Ralph Kramden, the volatile-yet-lovable, hard-luck bus driver tries to learn golf to impress his boss and get the promotion and raise that would never come. YouTube it. . .a few giggles guaranteed!

In 1972 **The Jackie Gleason Inverrary Classic** replaced The National Airlines Open Invitational. it was among the richest events on tour with an inaugural purse of $260,000 and a $52,000 winner's share. The regular event was not played in 1976, as Inverrary hosted the Tournament Players Championship in late February, won by Jack

Nicklaus. Gleason's nine-year affiliation ended after 1980, but the event continued at Inverrary through 1983. It moved to the TPC Eagle Trace in Coral Springs in 1984 for eight editions.

From 1992 to 1995, the event was held at the Weston Hills Golf & Country Club in Weston. It then returned to Coral Springs, first at the TPC at Eagle Trace in 1996 and then at the TPC at Heron Bay from 1997 to 2002. In 2003, the event moved to Palm Beach Gardens, first at the Country Club at Mirasol through 2006, then began its current run at PGA National Golf Club's Champion Course in 2007. Since 2007, the tournament's main beneficiary is the Nicklaus Children's Health Care Foundation, chaired by Barbara Nicklaus, wife of golf legend Jack Nicklaus.

His Memorial Mass was celebrated by His Excellency Bishop Norbert Dorsey who said, "Throughout his professional life (Jackie) kept the heart of a child. A whimsicalness that cheered up a sad and tired world." He is buried at St. Mary's Cemetery in a lavish above-ground mausoleum. Etched into the marble stairway leading to his sarcophagus reads the inscription, "And Away We Go."

Dean Martin 1972-1975

Dean dropped out of Steubenville High School (Ohio) in the 10th grade because he thought he was smarter than his teachers. He bootlegged liquor, served as a speakeasy croupier, was a black-jack dealer, worked in a steel mill, and boxed as a welterweight. He billed himself as "Kid Crochet." prizefighting earned him a broken nose (later straightened), a scarred lip, many broken knuckles and a bruised body. Of his 12 bouts, he said: "I won all but 11."

An American singer, actor, comedian, and producer. One of the most popular and enduring American entertainers of the mid-20th century, Martin was nicknamed the "King of Cool" for his seemingly effortless charisma and self-assurance. He and Jerry Lewis formed the immensely popular comedy duo Martin and Lewis, with Martin serving as the straight man to Lewis' slapstick hijinks. Martin went on to become a star of concert stages, nightclubs, audio recordings, motion pictures, and television. He was also a member of the "Rat Pack".

Martin was the host of the television variety programs The Dean Martin Show and The Dean Martin Celebrity Roasts. His relaxed, warbling, crooning voice earned him dozens of hit singles.

The Tucson Open was a golf tournament in Arizona on the PGA Tour from 1945 to 2006, played annually in the winter in Tucson. The Conquistadores brought celebrity sponsorship to the Tournament in 1972 and with it, the first network broadcast. Singer Dean Martin was the first host to lend his name and gather his friends from the entertainment world to participate in the event. **The Dean Martin Tucson Open** was televised by NBC. The network's additional financial support, along with a contribution from the city, allowed the Conquistadores to increase the purse to $150,000. Martin continued as the celebrity host through 1975.

A typical Dean Martin day was an early round of golf, an afternoon of gin – the card game – and then dinner with the family. Afterwards, they'd watch television. "He didn't stay up late and carouse. When dad was there with Frank and Sammy and they did the whole Rat Pack (thing)...he'd hang out with them a little bit but other than that, normally it was no way. He just didn't want to. He would drink apple juice onstage when they would do that whole (drunk) bit," his daughter said of his reputation for drinking during performances. She said her father would often beg off a night of carousing with Sinatra and Sammy Davis Jr. – his Rat Pack buddies - in order to make an early tee time.

"Dean liked playing with really good golfers. He didn't play with hacks, because it made him better," Pavoni said. "And one guy was saying that Dean was a guy that everybody liked him -- guys liked him, girls liked him, he was the real deal. "He was a super nice guy. And he played golf all the time."

Sammy Davis, Jr 1973-1988

An American singer, musician, dancer, actor, vaudevillian and comedian. He was noted for his impressions of actors, musicians and other celebrities. At the age of three, Davis began his career in vaudeville with his father, Sammy Davis Sr. and the Will Mastin Trio, which toured nationally. After military service, Davis returned to the trio. Davis became an overnight sensation following a nightclub performance at Ciro's (in West Hollywood) after the 1951 Academy Awards. With the trio, he became a recording artist. In 1954, he lost his left eye in a car accident, and several years later, he converted to Judaism, finding commonalities between the oppression experienced by African-American and Jewish communities

Davis was a victim of racism throughout his life, particularly during the pre-Civil Rights era, and was a large financial supporter of the Civil Rights Movement. One day on a golf course with Jack Benny, he was asked what his handicap was. "Handicap?" he replied, "Talk about a handicap. . .I'm a one-eyed Negro Jew." This was to become a signature comment, recounted in his autobiography and in countless articles.

The tournament was founded in 1952 as the Insurance City Open, it was renamed the Greater Hartford Open in 1967, a title that was retained through 2003. **The Sammy Davis Jr. Greater Hartford Open** (1973-84), **the Canon Sammy Davis Jr. Greater Hartford Open** (1985-88). Officials said when Davis became involved in the event, he helped increase the pro-am celebrity attendance from 2,000 to 40,000 and the tournament's purse has risen from $200,000 to $700,000. Other iterations of the tournament:1989-2002 the tournament was held as the Cannon Greater Hartford Open, 2003 as the Greater Hartford Open, 2004-2006 as the Buick Championship and 2007 to the time of this publication, The Travelers Championship.

Sammy Davis Jr., "a golf nut for the last 20 years," said, "he was honored to be the first black person to have a Professional Golfers' Association tournament named after him. I hope the tournament will encourage more black youngsters to take up the game. Some kid may say if they can name a tournament after a black celebrity maybe some day they'll name one after me. Just as some kid who sees Arthur Ashe playing tennis may want to try tennis. I hope in some small way to do for golf what Jackie Robinson and Arthur Ashe have done for their sports."

Other celebrities who have lent their names to support various tournaments

Roy Clark	Champions Tour	Tulsa, Okla	1984
Joe Garagiola	PGA Tour	Tucson, Ariz	1977-83
Gatlin Brothers	Champions Tour	Reno, Nev	1983-84
Gatlin Brothers	Champions Tour	Abilene, Texas	1989-90
Gatlin Brothers	PGA Tour	Abilene, Texas	1988
Wayne Gretzky	Nationwide Tour	Ontario, Canada	2008
Johnny Mathis	Champions Tour	LosAngeles	1986
Ed McMahon	PGA Tour	Moline, Ill.	1975-79
Charley Pride	Champions Tour	Albuquerque, N.M.	1987-91
Justin Timberlake	PGA Tour	Las Vegas	2008-12

Northern California circa 1966

Northern California has the richest golf tradition of any geo-graphical pocket this side of Scotland…a virtual spawning ground for professional and amateur champions. There are 9 golf courses designed by Alistar MacKenzie in the area. One of two places on earth with a Mediterranean climate, it is truly one of God's special places on earth.

In 1966, the cultural and political upheavals of the 1960's were taking shape. In January about 8,000 U.S. soldiers land in South Vietnam; the war was ramping up (U.S. troops now totaled 190,000), the racially benighted times in the United States was growing, Negros were becoming African Americans and demanding equality. In February, Nancy Sinatra's "These Boots are Made for Walking" hit #1 on the U.S. Billboard Hot 100 Chart. In March, the *London Evening Standard* published an interview with John Lennon that became an enduring part of the Beatles' legacy. "We're more popular than Jesus now," Lennon told the rock journalist Maureen Cleave. "I don't know which will go first—rock 'n' roll or Christianity." The Texas Western Miners defeat the Kentucky Wildcats with 5 African-American starters, ushering in desegregation in athletic recruiting.

1966 was Muhammed Ali's busiest as heavyweight champion; comprising five fights. He also went 15 rounds for the first time in his career. He seemed bulletproof. He took the sport he loved to new heights (and like the Beatles, took the American consciousness along with it). He set a benchmark for heavyweight combat that will never be matched. The Greatest was at his greatest…at his absolute peak - you can't hit what you can't see, never taking a backward step in defeating George Chuvalo in March, less than 2 months later in May, a sixth round TKO'ing of Henry Cooper, in August, a third round knockout by Ali of Brian London in London! The Beatles played their final concert on August 29th at Candlestick Park. A twelve round TKO of Karl Mindenberg in September (three firsts in this fight: the first lefthander Ali faced professionally, the first southpaw to fight for the heavyweight title & first heavyweight fight on German soil), This fight also displayed the kind of character that permeated Muhammed Ali's soul: referee Teddy Waltham(a caucasian) was relieved of his earnings for officiating that night by a pickpocket. Upon hearing the news, Ali was disappointed and decided to help the Englishman, who was understandably distraught. Mickey Duff recalls, "(Ali) asked somebody how much a thousand pounds was in American money, went into his own pocket and gave it to Waltham".

In November, Cleveland Williams unfortunately met with the debut of the Ali shuffle. Floating like a butterfly, stinging like a bee, this fistic masterpiece is where The Greatest displayed his full repertoire and took virtually nothing in return. Referee Harry Kessler halted the slaughter at 1:08 in the third round. Many believe it was Ali at his zenith. It was soon to be interrupted for three years while he fought courts over his refusal, unlike former Heavyweight Champion Joe Louis, to be drafted into the U.S. Army. Ali was stripped of his heavyweight title on April 28, 1967. (Ali would later have his conscientious objector status upheld by the U.S. Supreme Court and resumed fighting in 1970), "The man who has no imagination has no wings."

On November 9th, cupids arrow hit John Lennon's heart for Yoko Ono. On December 15th, Walt Disney dies while producing *The Jungle Book*, the last animated feature under his personal supervision. 1966 also brought Frank Sinatra a Grammy for Album of the Year - September of My Years – and Steve Jeros, our neighbor, a job picking up golf balls at the nearby driving range. It was the '60's man and a couple of more bodies were needed to pick up golf balls - not by motorized cart, mind you, but by hand with metal scoops attached to golf shafts. Guido (my twin brother) and I were just fourteen but told Rig Ballard, owner of prosaic but rhytmic named Airways Fairways Driving Range, we were sixteen. He hired us on the spot for $1.10 per hour plus perks. Perks included hitting all the golf ball we wanted and free golf lessons on Saturdays by the teaching professional, Lucious Bateman.

Lucious Bateman

An African American male, born in Louisiana in 1906, grew up in Biloxi, Mississippi. As a young man worked at the nearby Edgewater Hotel and Golf Club. Where, as a caddy, he could be found teeing up golf balls during lessons for the head golf professional, Art Saunders. "I'd watch and listen 'cause I was so close." Eventually, Lucious rose to the rank of head caddy. Playing privileges were extended and at one time, Lucious owned the course record at three under par. The 1940s in the South was not the place to be a man of color. After witnessing his best friend dragged on the highway for dating a white woman, he headed west. "I had a sister in Oakland, California, so I just picked up and moved." She had a small two-bedroom house on Seventy-seventh Avenue where they lived until his death in April of 1972.

Working nights at the shipyards for Bethlehem Steel left mornings or afternoon hours for golf. Alameda Muni was across the tracks past the Southern Pacific depot, down on the mudflats of the western shore of the San Francisco Bay. It was during the mid-1940s that Bateman honed his game. "I could shoot in the '60s every day." The first black football player, Marion Motley, took the field in 1946, Jackie Robinson first played for the Brooklyn Dodgers in 1947, but it wasn't until 1962 that Charlie Sifford was allowed to join the professional golfers tour. Of course, that didn't stop Charlie Sifford (the first African American inducted into the golf hall of fame in St. Augustine, Florida—November 15, 2004) from following the tour around the country. The Caucasians were playing Claremont Country Club for the Oakland Open Championship, and Charlie stopped at nearby Alameda Muni for a little action. Bateman, his game as sound as a Roosevelt dollar, obliged Charlie for three fives. At the end of 18 holes Lucious was the victor. However, when it came time to collect, Charlie stiffed him! Although Bateman understood, better than most, the battle that Charlie had chosen, he reminded him of his debt every time he saw him in the ensuing years.

By 1949, Bateman was offered a job at Airway Fairways Driving Range, "mostly as a handyman," to pro Bob Fry. Located across from the Oakland Airport, Bateman would clean range balls, repair equipment, and, during his free time, teach kids. Tony Lema said in a 1965 *Golf Digest* article about Bateman, "Many kids might have made jails instead of pars and birdies if it hadn't been for Loosh." "Bateman had a touch." John McMullin, 1956 PGA Rookie of the Year said, "He could see something when it broke down and he could fix it easily. And he was a motivator. One time I got upset while playing and he just walked off the golf course. He didn't tolerate a bad attitude. He did not have a good car and he lived in a shack, but me and a lot of the other kids never had to pay." "He was one of a kind. Dick and I would go up after high school", said John Lotz, who won the 1971 Concord Open. "And we'd pick up balls at the range. Then Lucious would work on our games."

"Kids who were on the borderline of society from being good boys or bad boys, he helped through their adolescence," said Dick Lotz. "There were kids he gave jobs to that had been in juvenile hall. He guided them to be good citizens. I think that is probably the more important thing about him than the golf aspect. I look at what the First Tee (youth golf program) represents and its nine core values, and I think, 'Man, Lucius invented 'em.'"

Further proof of Bateman's playing ability came in 1945 when the reigning heavyweight champion, Joe Louis—who at the time was the national spokesman for the US Army—was barnstorming across the country raising money for war bonds. Late in the fall of 1945, the champ's schedule brought him to San Francisco to stage a boxing exhibition with Sugar Lip Anderson and Big Boy Brown. Golf, being the champ's favorite pastime, had scheduled an exhibition match at Harding Park Golf Course. Bateman, being one of the better African American players in the area, was in the feature foursome with the champ.

His legacy as a teacher of golf and moral lessons to hundreds of young boys—almost all of them white—is undeniable and perhaps even more powerful in an age where generosity of spirit is so hard to come by. Many of Bateman's pupils became *champions in life* as a result of the guidance they received from a man who pretty much worked from sunup to sundown six days a week.

In Bateman's course from caddy, to range hand, to golf instructor, he cultivated an almost mystical communion with his students. He followed no formulas, no regimens, no superstitious rituals. The wisdom he harbored was time tested. He approached each student as a distinct individual and followed his own hunches and experiences. Students blossomed under his tutelage. By instinct or by study, Lucious had an exceptionally firm grasp of human imagination and very opinionated as to what the golf swing should look like or more importantly, *feel* like. Bateman's reputation proved, and his students knew, that if you believed in what his years of experience detected and practiced his cures, your shot making ability would improve and most likely your scores.

Golf Lessons from the Six Under Par Club

Lucious Bateman – Golf Instructor Airway Fairways Driving Range, Oakland, California

There were two types of students in Lucious's eyes: his "boys" and the paying public. "I don't believe in remaking a golfer. I try to take what he has had and make some good out of it. I usually advise a reasonably short backswing, but even then it depends on the pupil's physical capabilities." To those he instructed who had no physical liabilities, a compact backswing was encouraged. All his "boys" had a full shoulder turn and *loaded the angle* on the downswing. His theory was that there should be little or no wrist break on the backswing (or as McMullin would say, "When your shoulders stop turning, your hands and arms stop moving") and the wrist break should occur when the lower body initiates the downswing. Another one of his pet peeves was seeing a player with the face shut at the top of the backswing. He called it *rat foot*—although Arnold Palmer, Billy Casper, and Lee Trevino did okay with it. A big no-no in his book, he felt that the hands should "pronate" (release) through the shot. He would demonstrate this with his left hand, palm facing skyward, "pay me" or contrasting by pulling his left hand out of his pants pocket with his wrist bowed toward you, "pay you." The "pay you" action is what the left wrist must look like at impact to produce a straight or slightly drawing shot when the face is shut at the top of the backswing—and what your left hand looked like, reaching into your pocket, gathering money to pay off a bet. Although there have been many major championships won by closed-to-square players.

We worked many hours on the takeaway. Bateman would place tees in the ground approximately eight inches behind my takeaway path, whether he wanted the club to come a little more inside or outside … it depended on my existing takeaway path. The downswing was always initiated with the lower body. Bateman demonstrated this by facing you, where he would pull on the outside of your left pants pocket with his right hand while holding the butt end of the club with his left. Additionally, he would then have you hold on to the club "with both hands," then grab a hold of your wrists and demonstrate how the lower body drags the butt end of the club toward the ball (shades of McDonald Smith) and how the release works.

This is a mirror (face position at right hip level on the backswing—square) of that (face position at left hip level on downswing—closed). You had to get "a feel for it." On the finish, always have your belly button facing the target. He strongly advocated to beginners to "swing the club from the inside out."

I watched Bateman give many, many golf lessons. A few of his favorite sayings, usually sprinkled in with the lessons …

"If it feels short and tight, it's right."

"Short irons were made to hit short."

"This is a mirror of that."

"Your feet can feel."

"If it's not one thing, it's another."

"He putts like a one-eyed sheriff."

"Horse that runs fast don't last."

"What goes around comes around."

"Still hog drinks the slop."

"Just cuz someone is showing their ass doesn't mean you have to show yours."

Bateman taught many a junior to play great golf with little remuneration. He died a poor man in the quiet glory of a driving range pro but left behind a rich legacy of wisdom to many great players. The driving range at Chuck Corcia Golf Complex at Alameda, California, is dedicated to Bateman. There a plaque reads,

"This driving range is dedicated to a man who devoted his life to the game of golf and shared it with everyone he came in contact with, especially kids. He taught kids both the physical and mental aspects of golf and life. A true sportsman at all times. 1979."

Lucious Bateman was elected an honorary member of the Northern California Professional Golfers Association at the October 22, 2008, board of directors meeting. As the eleventh recipient of this prestigious award in Section's 88 year history, the honorary membership highlights the outstanding accomplishments and achievements Lucious has earned in the game of golf in Northern California and Western Nevada, focusing on his contributions and participation beginning at the grassroots level.

This is a list of players Bateman instructed who played the PGA Tour sometime between the mid-1950s to the early 1970s.

Tony Lema	John McMullen	Dick Lotz
Don Whitt	John Lotz	Bob Boldt
Ross Randle		

In contrast to what Bateman taught some club "rat footers" who have won major championships. It's impact that counts.

Arnold Palmer

Billy Casper

Photos by Chuck Brenkus

Lee Trevino

John Geertsen Sr. - Golf Professional, San Francisco Golf Club, San Francisco, California

John Geertsen was a great player—a former touring professional and winner of the 1940 Crosby Pro-Amateur (with amateur Russell Osgood). He was also an excellent instructor having tutored Tony Lema (my and many of my friends boyhood idol), Johnny Miller, Ray Leach, and John Abendroth. Tony Lema grew up in my home town, San Leandro, California. Thinking it would be prudent to follow the same path as Tony Lema (Tony worked as an assistant at the San Francisco Club when John Geertsen was the head professional), an appointment was set to have Mr. Geertsen look at my swing. Once Bateman got wind of this, he was furious. Bateman had issues with other instructors "stealing" his best players and then taking credit for their good golf. The forty-five-minute lesson was fascinating. It was a total deviation from what Bateman prescribed about the takeaway. Geertsen was a proponent of "setting the angle early." Meaning that as the club is coming away from the ball, there is an angle set that has the shaft pointing perpendicular (straight up) from the ground at hip height. Whereas, Bateman was a proponent of a "one-piece takeaway"—the shaft parallel to the ground at hip high. He hated the fact that he now had to explain to me why I shouldn't be setting the angle early. Either way works as long as the lower body is dragging the butt end of the club into the hitting zone.

Notice the position of Johnnie Miller's hands ... compare "club rat foot's" hand position at the same stage of the swing. You'll find those in "club rat foot" need to hold and drag the clubface ("pay you") though impact a little longer.

John McMullen - Golf Instructor, Palo Alto Muni, Palo Alto, California

When Bateman first laid eyes on John, his uncles were trying to teach him how to play golf. Frustrated with their lack of success, they turned to Bateman for help. Immediately, he took John's long, loopy swing and made him stop moving his hands when his shoulders stopped. In less than seven months, John went from a guy who could barely break 100 to a 70s shooter. Within a year, John was shooting in the 60s and winning the NorCal Junior. Eventually, John tried his luck on the PGA tour becoming the rookie of the year in 1956. A story that Bateman used to tell about McMullen ... John, who was good enough to have wasted a seven-shot lead in the 1958 Dallas Open (precursor to Byron Nelson Invitational)—that later led to a sudden death playoff with he, Gary Player, Sam Snead, and Julius Boros (Sam Snead was the eventual winner)—had come off the tour to work on his swing.

During the 1950s, players were not as friendly toward one another as they are today. Purses were smaller. It was survival of the fittest. Payouts in the tournaments were to the top 25 players only. A group of players somehow convinced John that if he could drive it within a few yards of George Bayer (former lineman with the Chicago Bears and at the time the longest hitter on tour) with a half swing (when the shoulders stop turning the hands stop moving) that, with a full swing, he could knock it by him. Out went Bateman and McMullin to play the front side of the South Course at Chick Corcia Golf Complex. McMullen shot 32, eagling both par fives. Upon completion of the round, Bateman asked John, "Why would you want to change your swing, you just shot 32?" To which McMullen replied, "So I can hit irons to the 5 pars." John had hit fairway woods into those 5 pars ...

John was a great player who lost his nerve on the putting green. We once witnessed him at the 1967 Charles Schulz "Peanuts" Pro Am, putting with his eyes closed, bogey the last hole to lose the event. Unlike Ralph Gudahl, John was someone who knew how to strike the ball and verbalize how to do it. His theory "when the shoulders stop the hands stop" made complete sense about the backswing. Check out Tiger Wood's swing. When his shoulders stop turning, do his hands keep moving? No!

The real awakening came when I questioned John of the whys of a poorly struck shot. "Work from the ball back," answered John. Meaning that if I wanted to hit a high fade and ended up hitting a low draw, I needed to examine impact. What position did I need to change to get into the position to hit a high fade? And to find out what prohibited me from doing so. John also taught me about the "release fade" (releasing your hands through impact and having the ball spin left to right . . . something Johnnie Miller practiced to perfection), the difference between being a hands player vs. being a shoulder and hips player. It was through these epiphanies with John that the realization to change my swing feels in order to become a more consistent player was paramount. John embodied the Bateman spirit.

Don Baucom – Baucom's House of Golf, San Leandro, California

Oftentimes Bateman would take Guido and me around to the NCGA amateur events to watch his horses play, always pointing out what he liked or didn't like (as previously stated, he hated seeing the face shut at the top of the backswing) about whoever we were watching. That particular day we had gone out to see Bob Kessler play in the 1967 Hayward City Amateur. "Watch how still ol' Kessler keeps his head." It is where we first met Don Baucom.

Don was a hardworking, earnest, fun guy who probably played three hundred rounds of golf with Bateman. Baucom, who grew up in Oakland, met Bateman as a teenager when he went to work in 1951 as Airway Fairways shagging balls. "The group of kids who hung out there, every Friday we'd go golf with Lucious. Being that I didn't have any money, he'd play green fees, get you clubs and balls, pick up the tab for your meal, and he never asked for anything in return. He would shoot in the 60s every single day. I saw Bateman shoot 29 at least three times."

Working part-time as a mechanic at a service station, Don's full-time job was driving a big rig for the Teamsters. Somehow he managed to squeeze in a few rounds of golf. At that point in his life, Baucom was looking to make money to set up his retirement. Eventually, Don took a leave of absence from the Teamsters and started to come around the driving range to work on his game. We played many rounds of golf together. Whether it was partnering in the Northern California Golf Association 2-Ball Championship or playing in high stakes games with his pigeons (or as he liked to call them, with his French accent, peee-johns). Baucom bank rolled our action. Those types of environments is where you learn a ton about yourself and how you perform with the heat cranked up.

In April of 1972, after Bateman had had his final, fatal stroke, we went to the hospital to see Bateman. Don came out of the ICU and told us, "I saw my daddy die and I'm telling you, you ain't gonna see him alive again. Better go say good-bye."

After Bateman's death, Don leased the driving range from Lee Duggan, renaming it Baucom's House of Golf. Don taught me a great deal about life and always looked out for my best interests. Like a big brother, nobody messed with me when Baucom was around.

Currently teaching golf in the Sacramento area, many of his students have sent in applications on his behalf to various golf publications recommending him as one of the top teaching professionals in the country. Don's been Kevin Sutherland's (Mr. 59 Sr.) teacher for over thirty years. "Golf was a different game then, played with different equipment. The game has changed so much because of the equipment. Short, heavy, 43.5-inch long True Temper Dynamic Gold steel-shafted persimmon-headed drivers that hit a wound ball that spun like a top have been replaced with graphite-shafted metal-headed drivers (about twice the size of the persimmon headed drivers), that measure two inches longer and have half the swing weight. And it is not just the driver; it is the whole equipment revolution.

There are many more good players today because of the equipment—the driver and the ball, in particular.

"Ol' Bateman's contempt for that 'rat foot' at the top of the swing is passé. Now it's let-it-release-draws or hold-fades. Many of the top players show two knuckles with their left hand grips. Check out Palmer, Casper, and Trevino, all of them held the face square through impact—the longer the better. Hogan held the face square through impact six to seven inches—more than any other player (Snead, six inches; Nelson five inches). Now called the smash factor—it's is the measurement of how long the clubface is square through impact and the ball's speed coming off the clubface." Don Baucom

A device many instructors now teach with a camera that is called the Trac Man.

It measures these 10 aspects of your swing:

Clubhead speed
Ball speed
Smash factor
Launch
Spin
Angle of attack
Path angle
Clubface angle

Carry

Total yardage

Video? Don will video to look at the problem. Don uses an app—V1 Golf—and/or a GL7 camera that can slow the swing down to 15,000 to one frames. You swing the club . . . the ball flight in the air tells you all you really need to know.

Baucom knew Bateman best and it's reflective of the success he's had as a golf instructor. A great role model who believed that a positive attitude is a must for life. Why not enjoy life to the fullest? And have some fun while you can.

Talbert Smith - Golf Professional Claremont Country Club, Oakland, CA

Digressing with some facts about Claremont Country Club— in the fall of 1925, Alistar MacKenzie arrived in California to prepare to redesign the Claremont Country Club, home course to his friend and well known Scottish professional golfer Macdonald Smith ("All you do is wind up—then unwind"). It was believed that Smith was partially responsible for luring MacKenzie to California and introducing him to several potential clients. The list of golf courses Alistar MacKenzie designed in Northern California:

1927	Meadow Club	Fairfax
	Redlands Country Club	Redlands
1928	Valley Club of Montecito	Santa Barbara
	Cypress Pt. Club	Pebble Beach
	Northwood Golf Club	Monte Rio
1929	Pasatiempo Golf Club	Santa Cruz
	Claremont Country Club	Oakland
1930	Green Hills Country Club	Milbrae
1932	Sharp Park Golf Course	Pacifica
	Haggin Oaks Golf Complex	Sacramento

In 1937, Sam Snead's first full year on the Tour, he won five events, including the Oakland Open at Claremont Country Club. This was also the tournament in 1937 where Hogan, leaving his hotel for the final round found his car jacked up on milk crates and all four of his tires gone. If Hogan hadn't taken fifth place prize money ($285) in the 1937 tournament he had vowed to hang up his spikes. The 1938 through 1944 Oakland Open's (World War II cancelled the event in 1943) were played at Sequoyah Country Club.

Throughout the 1940–1960s Tal Smith (no relation to MacDonald Smith) was one of Northern California's finest players. Winning the Alameda Commuters in 1941, 1946, 1947, 1950, 1951, 1952, and 1954, the Northern California Open in 1947, the San Francisco City in 1957—Tal had one of the best short games in the history of Northern California Golf. Bateman once told me that he witnessed Tal seemingly shank almost every iron shot yet managed to shoot around par. As Bobby Locke would say, "The secret of golf is turning three shots into two." Tal had that reputation and a fabulous array of feel shots . . . he was a magician around the greens! His advice was sought about the short game. Our only lesson occurred late one autumn afternoon around the 18th green at Claremont Country Club. Some notes from my diary:

*   Posture perfect . . . right palm
*   Lob shot - requires speed through impact - follow through with your head back until ball hits the green.
*   All clubs are toe heavy, lead with the heel (shades of McDonald Smith)
*   Knees on short shots judge distance
*   "Feel the ball come up the clubface. All these shots around the green have a different feel to them. Look, this lob shot has a totally different feel than this running 6 iron. Search out those feels and remember them." Talbert Smith

Art Bell – Teaching Professional Pebble Beach Golf Links, Pebble Beach, California

Art was a great player for three decades and famous friends of Der Bingle (Bing Crosby).

Art won the Crosby Pro Am in 1938 with Phillip Finlay at Rancho Santa Fe (site of the first few Crosby's) and again at Pebble Beach in 1952 with Bill Hoelle where they were co-winners with Bob Toski and Dr. Bob Knudson. In the 1946 PGA Championship (only

Byron Nelson was exempt from the PGA's grueling thirty-six hole Monday and Tuesday qualifier) Art qualified but was demolished in the sweet sixteen round, 5 and 4 by Ben Hogan. Hogan (weighing in at 137 pounds) eventually won his first major championship beating Porky Oliver (weighing in at 220 pounds).

The California Golf Club in South San Francisco, holds their annual member-guest named after Art, the "Cat's Paw" . . . imagine Art's reaction to the ball with the putter head after missing a short putt, dragging the ball back with his left hand holding the putter head and attempting the putt again.

A lesson with Art was scheduled and we met at the far end of the old Pebble Beach driving range. After whacking out a few shots, Art asked me in his cantankerous voice, "Why am I watching you hit these shots? If I could hit it like that, I could shoot in the 60s right now. Let me see you hit it from 60 yards in."

Diary entry
I. Setup
Set up blade square
Left arm and club shaft form a straight line
Elbows tight

II. Swing
Good tight feeling at the top of the backswing
Short irons - compact, short backswing
Try to play a short chip shot guiding it and giving it its power entirely from the knees.
Elbows next to side at finish

III. Impact
Check divots especially the outside line
Ideal—shallow
Too deep—outside
Hips block—ball flies right
Stay on right side too long—ball flies left

Mental:
Concentrate on key
Thinking of the clubface while the swing is in motion
Heel leading toe—fade
Toe leading heel—draw

Facts: 6 iron to wedge—"low gear" half swing

Olin Dutra – Golf Instructor Pajaro Dunes Golf Club, Pajaro, California

Olin Dutra began competing professionally in 1924 and would ultimately win nineteen tournaments during his career. His most successful years as a professional were in the early 1930s when he captured the 1932 PGA Championship, 1934 US Open and played for the United States in the 1933 and 1935 Ryder Cup.

In the 1932 PGA Championship, Dutra played 196 holes and finished an astounding 19-under par, including his finish as low qualifier.

"Dutra is perhaps best remembered for his 1934 US Open win. While traveling to the tournament, Dutra became ill and lost fifteen pounds. After two rounds, he was eight strokes behind the leaders; after the third round, he was in 18th place. Remember, 36 holes were the norm for the final two rounds. Before the final round, Dutra had an attack of dysentery that forced him to snack on sugar cubes throughout the round. Dutra was still able to shoot a 72 to hold off Gene Sarazen and win by a single stroke. "What we all need is a cool head amongst the hazards like Olin Dutra's. Dutra once had to pass seventeen golfers in the home stretch to win the National Open, and he did it." Sam Snead.

Olin Dutra was in the winter of his life when we met for our only lesson. Born and raised on the Monterey Peninsula, he was teaching golf at a course sandwiched between Pasatiempo Golf Course in Santa Cruz to the north and Pebble Beach on the Monterey Penninsula to the south. The 1932 PGA champion and the 1934 US Open champion was still mentally sharp as a razor.

The first thing he said to me was, "I played in my first major championship at age 29, when Bobby Jones, age 28, played in his last."

After a few warm up swings Olin said, "there's no limit where you can go with that golf swing."

"Are there any tips you can give me about the setup?" "Yes", he replied. "With your irons, your head is over the ball, and with the woods, your head is behind the ball. When I hit my driver, I try to set the ball up just inside the crease that is created by my left shoulder and arm. My fairway woods, on my left ear, and my irons off my nose. Learn to hit past your chin."

"Your grip is most important. MacDonald Smith—you do know who MacDonald Smith is, don't you?" Being a student of the game, I said, "Of course I do. He was a player in the 20s and 30s who had no equal to ball striking. Putting? That was a different story."

"I'm impressed", he continued. "Very few of my students know who he is. MacDonald used to say to me, hit it with the butt end of the club."

He spoke of his US Open victory. "On the last nine I knew I could win if I shot 34. Aim, fire, and get the feel of the motion."

Other pearls of wisdom from the great champion . . .

"Images—good pictures—without them you're like a ship without a rudder."

"Muscles memory is a byproduct of repetition."

"Don't think about your swing."

Ben Doyle – Golf Instructor, Quail Lodge Golf Club, Carmel, California

Ben was a disciple of *The Golfing Machine*, a book written by Homer Kelly that is based on scientific principles covering physics and geometry of the golf swing. It is a systematic way of understanding the golf swing. Homer explained that he simply applied these age-old proven principles to the golf swing. And with that, *The Golfing Machine* was born. Ben took great satisfaction in seeing his pupils develop as players and human beings. He was a great man who loved teaching golf. Personally, these philosophy/teachings seemed too complex . . . "Flat load my feet so I can snap load my power package. That way I can amplify both lag and drag pressure through impact fix. As long as my number 2 power accumulator doesn't break down, I can reach maximum centripetal force with minimum pivotal resistance. The pivot is a utilization of multiply centers to produce a circular motion for generating centrifugal force on an adjusted plane plus the means and balances necessary to deliver a two line delivery path. Golf is a geometrically oriented layer force that involves a physical muscular thrust and the geometry of a circle. You can divide the golf swing into twenty-four basic components, each having twelve to fifteen variations."

Whereas, Hogan had eight fundamentals, Homer Kelly's system has twenty-four. One should note Ben has had success with many players using the Homer Kelly system. However, any student must have complete confidence in the system he/she is being taught or should move on. The system Ben Doyle taught was far different than what Bateman taught. However, this excerpt from the book *The Golfing Machine* regarding clubhead lag is magnificent . . . "Clubhead lag is the secret to golf. It is—or should be—always present during the down stroke from top to follow through. It is quite simple in itself but absolutely indispensable and has no substitute or compensation. It is quite elusive but if mastered, assures a respectable performance on the basis of feel alone. It is the chief tool of educated hands for sensing, metering and directing the clubhead. It is imperative in conservation of momentum." Homer Kelley.

E. Harvie Ward – Golf Instructor, Fry Brothers Golf Shop, San Francisco, California

As a boy growing up in the South, Harvie had modeled his swing after the fluid move of Sam Snead, and there were hopeful comparisons he would be another godlike amateur, the second coming of Bobby Jones. Harvie's skills on the golf course flowed through him so naturally and he won with such effortless ease, that game just didn't seem to take that much out of him. During the 1950s early '60s, failure and victory were one and the same to Harvie.

Harvie truly did play golf for the joy of competing and would have been crazy to turn pro and refuse the guaranteed living that beckoned from the business world. During E. Harvie's ascent to one of the premiere players in the country, the light still flickered that another amateur would rise above the professional ranks and win a major championship. The last amateur to win a major championship? Johnnie Goodman in 1933 (Might qualify with Byron Nelson's eleven consecutive tournament wins, Ted Williams's .409 batting average, Joe DiMaggio's 56 game-hitting streak, and Nate "Tiny" Archibald leading the NBA in assists and scoring in the same year— as records that won't be broken anytime soon). Both sides of the Atlantic had hopeful comparisons for Harvie to be the second coming of Bobby Jones. It was the great Bobby Jones who urged Harvie to travel to England in the summer of 1952 and play in the British Amateur. It was Jones and Clifford Roberts, after his victory in that same 1952 British Amateur, who made the extraordinary gesture that had seldom, if ever, been offered to anyone—a lifelong exemption to play in the Masters. In 1955, possibly the finest year of his amateur career, he finished eighth at the Masters, sixth in the US Open, and won the US Amateur. Harvie attained favorite-son status with Bobby Jones, rubbed elbows with Byron Nelson and Ben Hogan (it was E. Harvie, who recommended to Hogan a Scottish caddy that packed Hogan's bag when the "wee ice mon" won the 1953 British Open), and palled around with Bing Crosby and the Hollywood set . . . as they say in Las Vegas, Harvie had "juice."

E. Harvie's game was long gone by the time we hooked up. An old-timer, a fellow amateur who once played with E. Harvie during his rise and fall told me, "You wouldn't believe it was the same player." For twelve years he was bionic, then fell back to mediocrity. The reality was that E. Harvie had an extremely low tolerance for alcohol and a high tolerance for beautiful women. Where Walter Hagen could nurse a highball all evening long, two scotch rocks and E. Harvie was shit-faced. Along with the hangovers came bouts of insecurity. They fed off of one another until E. Harvie was a mere shadow of his former self. Without confidence in this game, you're toast. His course record 63 at the fabulous old Tillinghast-designed

San Francisco Club still stands in tribute to the confident player he once was. If you think about it, like all great players, E. Harvie played by feel (right brain), had it, then completely lost those feels . . . shades of Ralph Guhdahl and David Duval!

My lesson with E. Harvie was about putting. Let's face it, to win back to back US Amateur . and be one of the premiere players in the game for a decade or more, you have to make a few putts. Our lesson took place in an office building in downtown San Francisco where a net, a matt, and an Astroturf putting green were our only connection to the game. Harvie was a big proponent of a good grip. "It's essential for championship golf." Regarding the putting stroke, approach, and philosophies, it came to me something Bateman once told me about putting, "Putting is an individual operation." The two things that this author did take away from our lesson that day was one of Harvey's big putting keys, "When assessing the line, look for the lighthouse." A spot along the intended lines path and to set up to that lighthouse . . . and the importance of a good grip.

John Lotz – John Lotz Golf Range, Los Gatos, California

John was a tremendously talented, highly volatile athlete, earning his block A from Arroyo High School in San Lorenzo, California, in wrestling, football, baseball, basketball, and golf. Where his temper may have funneled his focus to his advantage on the baseball diamond, the gridiron, the wrestling mat and on the basketball court . . . on the golf course, his temper was his worst enemy. Like any negative energy, it will eventually came back to haunt you. For a very long time, despite John's mental state—teetering between his insane temper and brilliance—he could flat out play. He won the Western Intercollegiate in 1961,1962, and 1963 (was also the NCGA Medalist those three years), improving his score by one shot in victory each year.

In the finals of the 1961 California State Amateur Championship, John had the eventual winner, John Richardson, 4 down after 21 holes. The fourth tee at Pebble Beach has a majestic view of Still Water Cove and up on the bluff, the 6th green. Walking along the fairway, he looked out on the beauty and said to himself, "I'm the 1961 California State Amateur Champion." He then proceeded to lose the championship (talk about the left-brain taking over!). The next year at the annual North/South matches—the top amateurs from Southern California play the top amateurs from Northern California—John, representing the Northern California Golf Association, was paired against the same man, John Richardson, who had defeated him just eleven months prior for the amateur title. The match play event was held at The Cypress Point Club. Hotter than a smoking 357 magnum, John, by the 11th hole had John Richardson out. Richardson was one under through 11 and defeated 8 and 7! John spent 7 years on the pro circuit and appeared to be on the verge of breaking into big money in 1972 when he was stricken by encephalitis on the eve of a Florida tournament.

At a point in my life, where my game was in a terrible funk, belongings packed headed south to Los Gatos, where John was building a driving range. Initially, John was as rude and obnoxious as anybody I'd ever met. Tired of what Bateman used to call "fairway buddies"—people that would suck up to you when you were going good but wanted nothing to do with you when you were going sideways—he saw me as a leech, trying to extract what he had taken a lifetime to learn, without paying the price. Because of my Bateman connection—and the fact that Guido and I helped bury Bateman—he gave me the smallest of windows to crawl through. My offer was to help him build out his driving range for all the golf balls one could hit. When he felt that my hard work equaled a golf lesson, he would give me one. Building my own tee box, sodding my own grass, a claim was laid to a spot where I could practice. The first time he watched me hit balls, he was thoroughly disgusted. "Look at those divots—way too deep. You need shallow divots on all iron shots. Get your elbows together. Become a tight, compact swinger. You really ought to work on pausing on every swing."

"Every swing?" I asked.

"Every swing." was his reply.

John was a big proponent of practice. Muscle memory was his way. Practice until the blisters bled. "Pictures, feelings, abstracts. That's how you play tournament golf." he would say. "But don't take it from me. That's something Gary Player said to me when I played with him. You cannot act on maybe. You must will what you will do. Otherwise you are no artist, you are an accident."

We often talked about the trilogy—mind, body, spirit . . . and it's constant movement, its struggles. Life is all in your perspective.

In November of 1984 on a fishing trip in the Sierra's, John lost his footing and fell into the fast flowing Trinity River. Several months later a jawbone was discovered, positive dental records what remained of John. He was 43.

Jim Langley – Head Professional, Cypress Point Club, Pebble Beach, California

In the fall of 1987, Jim was driving to a Pro Am at the San Francisco Golf Club with Bill Borland, then club president of Cypress Point. The car, due to a faulty fuel gauge, ran out of gas. Jim got out to push the car in the wee hours of the morning. Just as they arrived at the exit ramp, they were struck by another auto traveling at 50 mph. The impact momentarily trapped Jim's legs between both cars' bumpers and then threw him off the side of the road. "I just remember waking up in the hospital. My legs were broken and swollen four to five times their normal size. I didn't think much about my arm, but I learned later on I had pretty extensive nerve damage there."

As the fourth head golf professional at the Cypress Point Club—the other three being Adrian Wilson, for all of six months while the course was being completed; Jack Morris from 1928 to 1930; then Henry Puget from 1931 to 1971—he was in a brand-new arena with his handicap. Having been the sixth man of Pete Newell's 1959 University of California NCAA National Championship team, playing the tour from 1965 to 1970, he was well aware of how quickly things change in life.

My first round of golf with Mr. Langley was at Guido's Golf for Kids event. He was making his debut as the Pete Gray of professional golf. Playing one handed (as a right hander using his left arm), he honed his skills. Having played many rounds with one of his protégés, Eric Batten, we often spoke of Jim's sterling character, of his reputation and stature in the community. Jim and I had commonality: life, golf, basketball, and John Lotz. He'd run in marathons with John, shared the successes and disappointments of the tour life. He was one of the few individuals who recognized John's genius. Golf history–wise, we were locked in the same time warp—Bill Melhorn, Olin Dutra, MacDonald Smith, Alister MacKenzie, Ben Hogan, and Mike Souchek. We both had eaten our share of humble pie—albeit on two different levels—but now Jim was faced with a full-scale banquet. Jim, never one to change himself in order to change somebody else's impressions, treated the caddies with the same respect as a member of the senate.

A bit self-conscious when we started, what an inspiration he was to not only those playing in the tournament but the spectators as well. It wasn't that easy playing with one arm quasi-competitively. Nonetheless, on the old par 5, 9th at MPC's Dunes Course, he hit driver, 3 wood, 5 wood, and ever so nonchalantly rolled in his left to right breaking fifteen-footer for a birdie.

As the years passed, good fortune smiled upon me and was blessed to have played a few rounds with Mr. Langley at the majestic Cypress Point Club with an assortment of characters. We played a modified scotch twosome: on the first hole we all hit drives, then selecting the best tee shot, we played alternate shots from there on in. The par 3s were played with your own ball (scores combined) and then who hit off the following tee was determined by what had happened on the hole proceeding the par 3. With our skill level, breaking a hundred was challenging but the stroll merited so many great memories, beautiful scenery, and belly laughs. Jim was a saint.

Jim never charged for a golf lesson at Cypress Point. His respect for the membership was always at the forefront, along with his deep commitment to "give back." One aspect of the golf swing that we talked about on a number of occasions was what he considered an essential part of the golf swing—the weight transfer. "Balance creates rhythm and timing."

Dean James – Director of Golf Oakmont Golf Club, Santa Rosa, California

As it was learned from my two years working with Dean, most country clubs are ripe with politicking. The general manager, head golf professional and the superintendent's job security at any club rides on his/her personality and being able to mesh with the personality of the next chairperson on the board of directors. You could spend four years being the greatest guy on earth, and be without a job next month if the new chairperson thought you were an idiot. Fortunately, Dean possessed adroit personality skills where he was able to adjust to who was in charge . . . and he did it with such enthusiasm and vigor that no one recognized how he really felt. It's a testament to Dean's patience and his respect for his fellow man that led to Dean being the director of golf at Oakmont for some thirty years. Having seen so many old codgers take the big dirt nap, Dean often told me, "You die as you live . . . those that lived respectful, happy, peaceful lives died the same way." When he encountered "colorful characters," he was flexible enough to let the superficial stuff flow off him like water off a duck's back. He knew sooner or later that what goes around comes around.

Dean was big buddies with Charles Schulz, the creator of *Peanuts*. When the great cartoonist came to play, Dean always left one spot open for the boys in the shop. We all rotated playing with Dean, Dean's brother Larry (who many claim inspired the Pig Pen character), and Sparky. Pretty excited is an accurate assessment when my turn came around.

After our round, Dean invited me to the back of the driving range for a private lesson. One of Dean's principals was rolling the ankles: roll your left ankle on the backswing and your right ankle on the downswing. He suggested doing it without a club. It's a great way to feel the weight transfer and rolling onto your left instep through impact helps you release the club properly.

Charles Schulz

My first question to Sparky (CS's nickname) was who were his heroes? "Sam Snead, Ted Williams, and Billy Jean King," was his reply. Sparky was a brilliant man and did so much for the Redwood Empire that listing his contributions would take an entire chapter.

Charles Schulz's Philosophy

You don't have to actually answer the questions.
1.   Name the five wealthiest people in the world.
2.   Name the last five Heisman trophy winners.
3.   Name the last five winners of the Miss America Contest.
4.   Name ten people who have won the Nobel or Pulitzer Prize.
5.   Name the last half-dozen Academy Award winners for best actor and actress.
6.   Name the last decade's worth of World Series winners.

How did you do?

The point is, none of us remember the headliners of yesterday. They are not second-rate achievers. They are the best in their fields. But the applause dies. Awards tarnish. Achievements are forgotten. Accolades and certificates are buried with their owners.

Here's another quiz.
1.   List a few teachers who aided your journey through school.
2.   Name three friends who have helped you through a difficult time.
3.   Name five people who have taught you something worthwhile.
4.   Think of a few people who have made you feel appreciated and special.
5.   Think of five people you enjoy spending time with.

Easier?

The lesson: The people who make a difference in your life are *not* the ones with the most credentials, the most money, or the most awards. They are the ones who care.

"Don't worry about the world coming to an end today. It's already tomorrow in Australia." Charles Schultz.

Bob Boldt – Director of Golf Vintners Golf Club, Yountville, California

"Hollywood" (Arnold Palmer's nickname for Bob) was a sweet-strokin', slam-dunking, defensive-minded small forward from Berkeley High School (he's in their basketball and golf HOF) who received a basketball scholarship from the University of California in 1956. Unfortunately, he tore his ACL. In those days treatment was limited . . . what to do? His father, a member at Mira Vista Country Club in Richmond, California, invited the young row-bear out for an indoctrination to the world of golf. Impressed with the challenges the great game brings (and the beautiful women), he set his sights for stardom via the golf channel. Winning tournaments worldwide, smacking the little white sphere longer than any other senior player while crafting golf clubs for those "who beat his ass year in and year out," he finally had a bargaining chip for the questions that separated the champions from the also-rans. "This is information you won't read in *Golf Digest* or find down at your local drug store," Bob told me as my initial swings to our golf lesson began. He told me of his Bateman connection—most probably was the impetus for our chance meeting—but this author was extremely grateful nonetheless. It was an opportunity to meet with a great golfing mind to discuss the subtleties of the swing.

First up was the grip: "There are three main methods that are used in gripping the golf club: overlapping, interlocking, and the full-finger grip. The most popular grips are the overlapping (Vardon) and the interlocking. The overlapping and the interlocking grips are used not necessarily for hitting the ball farther but for better control of the clubhead during the swing and at impact. The full-finger grip releases the most power and, if used properly, the straightest shots. I have been playing and teaching the full-finger grip for over four decades, and I am convinced if all of the fingers are properly aligned, it is the best grip for any amateur or professional. There have been over sixty-two professional wins worldwide using the full-finger grip." For the record: Jimmy Demaret (1940, 1947, and 1950 Master's champion), Art Wall (1959 Master's champion. 45 aces!), Bob Rosburg (1959 PGA Champion), Moe Norman, and Beth Daniel (elected to the LPGA Hall of Fame in 1999 and World Golf Hall of Fame in 2000)—just to name a few. He also spoke of grip pressure (light but aggressive)—the pressure that's needed in holding the club.

Ten Finger Grip

If you are looking to hit the ball farther and with a straighter ball flight, the full-finger grip is for you. Fingers must be held close together and a long left thumb provides accuracy. Ten fingers (or eight fingers and two thumbs) produce longer straighter shots if your fingers are touching each other.

Use these simple guidelines
1. Do not change the basic hand position in your interlocking or overlapping grip
2. Simply move your right-hand fingers against your left forefinger.
3. The Vs in both your hands should be pointing up to your right shoulder.
4. A basic rule for your left hand is that if you cannot see its second knuckle when you look down your left hand is out of position.
5. Look down at your right hand and the V of your thumb and forefinger should point at your right shoulder.
6. Use a long left thumb with the right-hand fingers wrapping around the left thumb
7. You now have all your fingers releasing the clubhead in the hitting area. (In the overlap grip, the right-hand pinky and ring finger are inactivated; in the interlock the right-hand pinky and the left-hand forefinger are not even touching the club.)

He also spoke of "imaging a clock as your target with the intent of swinging at the twelve o'clock position. All the great players are thinking follow through as opposed to backswing."

"Inverse functioning?" I asked. He wasn't familiar with Percy Boomer jargon, but this author knew what he meant. Many instructors and students alike work on the backswing whereas thinking about the finish (and where to finish) is equally important.

What is inverse functioning?

"Consider the pivot. We have to teach you how to pivot by telling you or showing you how it is done and asking you to do it that way. That is, we teach it directly as if it were an end in itself. Yet, no good experienced golfer pivots directly like that - his pivot is the outcome of his correct conception of the follow through." Percy Boomer

"Now it is really important for you to get this difference in outlook or feeling clearly realized, because until you do, you cannot be anything but a mechanical golfer. So I will put the same thing to you in another way. When you watch a good golfer driving, you may feel that he has a perfect conception of the pivot, but you would probably be much nearer the truth in thinking that he had a perfect conception of the follow through." Percy Boomer

"In other words, again, his beautiful action has evolved not out of the study of how to turn his body but out of a feeling of how to swing past the ball." Percy Boomer

Funny story about Bob & Ben Hogan. . .Bob was good enough that he played on the PGA Tour & Senor Tour, once finishing in the top 5 at the Phoenix Open on the PGA tour. It was a water-shed event for him. It confirmed that he was a player and it inspired him to do whatever it took to get better. The biggest step he thought he could make was to seek out Ben Hogan to help him with his swing.

"No, you don't want to see Hogan," his friends said.

"Yeah, I do. I just had a good finish and I want to get better," he said.

"No, not Hogan," they warned.

"No, it's got to be Hogan," he persisted.

"Okay, if you say so," they acquiesced.

He called Colonial and arranged to meet with the great man a short time later. "Mr. Hogan will meet with you on Thursday," the shop said. Bob arrived at the appointed hour and the shop told him to head out to the range. Which he did. He warmed up and hit balls for hours, but Hogan never showed. "Come back tomorrow," the shop said.

Friday morning, he's on the range hitting balls and suddenly the great man is there. "Oh, Mr. Hogan, I'm so honored to get a chance to work with you. I just finished in the top five at the Phoenix Open and it would mean a great deal to me for you to take a look at my swing."

"Let me see you hit some shots," Hogan said. Bob started hitting balls while Hogan stood silently by. After he'd hit some shots, he looked expectantly over at Hogan. "I can't help you," was all he said and he turned and walked away.

At the Range

"The golf course in the midst of a round is no place to experiment or try anything new. The only place for that is the practice tee and Dad never went to the practice tee before a round." Bobby Jones.

"Before Ben Hogan started doing it," said Tommy "Thunder" Bolt, the flamboyant Arkansas shot maker and club thrower extraordinaire, who Hogan came to regard as one of his closest friends on the tour. "Nobody in their right mind regularly went to Misery Hill. That was our nickname for the practice tee, see, because that was where guys went to figure out what the hell was wrong with their swings. Hogan, on the other hand, went there to figure out what was *right* about his golf swing. Take it from me, brother, that was revolutionary! And by practicing as much as Ben did, which I swear was twice as much as anybody I ever saw, he basically reduced the margin for human error to damn near nothing. There was no shot he hadn't already hit a thousand times already out on Misery Hill. Nothing was ever a surprise to Ben Hogan in a golf tournament. That's the first thing that set him apart."

"It was inconceivable to think of Sam Snead or Bryon Nelson consulting a swing doctor or even asking another Tour professional for advice on their golf swings. As Ben Hogan later said, the answer was in the dirt, and pounding balls was the only way to find it. That was pretty much my father's attitude too. And it inevitably became mine." Arnold Palmer.

It is advisable to be professionally fitted with clubs, not only to get the lie and length right, but also for shaft flex, material (for example, graphite or steel, weight, grip thickness, and head design—each plays a role in controlling direction and maximizing distance). If you buy a set of clubs from an experienced club fitter to suit you and your swing, you will have increased your chances of playing to your potential. Good technique and correctly fitted clubs go hand in hand.

If you wish to change your technique, you need to blend mechanics and feel, and you must be able to switch from working on mechanics during practice to playing by feel on the course...especially rounds that count. You should work on only one or two thoughts or keys at a time, and work on trying to turn those thoughts, those keys into remembered feels, that you can place in your feeling storehouse.

More does not mean better. Take an idea or two out on the range and limit yourself to working on those aspects only. The swing is a linked action, and that it's important to work on the fundamentals. Always practice with a purpose. The big key—and what you're really trying to accomplish—is learning to hit better bad shots.

Who was the first player to pace yardage?

From Hogan, Jack Fleck picked up the habit of memorizing every feature of a hole's landscape, but he took his own preparations one step further by meticulously pacing off distances and compiling yardage books for later reference. "I used to tell people later that my memory just wasn't as good as Ben's." Fleck jokes. Many of his contemporaries point out that the lanky Iowan was among the first in tournament play to use a homemade yardage book, which Jack Nicklaus often gets credit for introducing to competitive play and which eventually became standard practice on tour.

Getting Started

Conceptually understand the grip, the triangle that's created with the arms and the how the shoulders wind the triangle . . . and how the lower body generates the power. "All you do is wind up then unwind." MacDonald Smith.

Chief feel number 1

"When your forward shoulder hits your chin, you're pretty much done with the backswing. Don't try for more than this. It's been said that Ben Hogan used to wear out his shirt at the point of the left shoulder because his backswing was so consistent that the same spot always hit his chin. He must have had a tough beard! Of course, he hit an awful lot of balls, too. The trigger for me was pinning that left shoulder up against the chin. Once I got there, I knew I was done with my backswing. Anything else after that was a wasted motion that bred inconsistency." Johnny Miller.

"Turning the left shoulder underneath your chin on the backswing. Get a feel of getting your left shoulder underneath your chin. Once your shoulders stop—your hands stop." John McMullen.

"Visualize the backswing plane as a large pane of glass that rests on the shoulders as it inclines upward for the ball. As the arms approach hip level on the backswing, they should be moving parallel with the plane and should remain parallel with the plane (just below the glass) to the top of the backswing. It would be ideal if the arms could be swung back parallel to the plane from the very start of the swing, but because of the way we human beings are constructed, a man gripping a club can't get his arm onto the plane until they are nearly hip high." Ben Hogan.

"The center of gravity of the body must stay in one place throughout the swing. That is, if a line is drawn through the nose or head to the ground, the head must stay in that position throughout the swing." Ben Hogan.

A checkpoint for a proper, true shoulder turn is that you should *feel* the left shoulder brushing your chin at the top of the backswing.

Chief feel number 2

"At the top of the backswing the groin muscle on the inside of your right leg near your right upper thigh will tighten. This subtle feeling of tightness there tells you that you have made the correct move back form the ball." Ben Hogan.

At the completion of your turn, your weight has shifted to the right but has remained inside the right foot, knee, and hip.

Chief feel number 3

"Always remember that your swing does not end at clubhead impact with the ball. You must hit completely through. The ball is hit from impact on through, and not to the ball. This holds true for all clubs. My hands are still firmly in control of the club at the finish of the swing. The supposition that the eyes must remain fixed throughout the follow through on the spot from which the ball was hit is completely erroneous. This is unnatural and retards the free and full turn of the shoulders." Byron Nelson.

Chief feel number 4
On the finish always have your belly button facing the target and the weight off your right foot.
Practice and try to get a feel for these 4 concepts. Once you understand impact—*how does the ball get into the air?*—you are on your way to becoming a better golfer. Review the "Impact" section especially Figure 6.

Range Drills
* Hit balls with left side only
  Turning and holding "billiard rack"—hands at waist high
  Turning and holding "billiard rack"—left shoulder under/ pressed under chin
* Practice release on short shots—pronation
  "This is a mirror of that"—backswing no longer than waist high
  Follow through no longer than waist high
* Hit balls with left hand and last three fingers of right hand— leaving thumb and forefinger off
* Hit balls while holding tee in fingers of right hand to prevent regripping
* Extension on follow through
* Drag right leg through the shot and touch left leg

Golf Workout
A golf workout used to involve taking a couple of practice swings and lightly limbering up your golf cart accelerator foot. But the days of "golf fitness" as an oxymoron ended when lean machines like Tiger Woods and David Duval started mauling their chubbier counterparts. Even old school vets like Greg Norman now log up to ten hours a week in the gym. "I don't lift like Arnold Schwarzenegger,"

allows the Shark. "But I do keep my muscles toned." His fitness consultant, Pete Dravotich, is more specific: "You need to get strong in the lower body to be explosive off the tee, strong in the trunk so your spine is stable during the swing, and strong in the shoulders and arms to limit repetitive-use injuries." Devised by Dr. Lewis Yocum, a noted sports physician who advises PGA pros, this workout can be done at home two or three times a week. Warm up with a five minute walk. For the stretches, find the limit of your comfort zone and hold that position for ten to fifteen seconds. Repeat each stretch two or three times. Do ten repetitions per set for the strength exercises, using two- to five-pound weights and progressing to three sets as you get stronger.

1. Posterior Shoulder Stretch: Grasp the back of your opposite elbow and pull it toward chin as far as you can. Repeat with the other elbow. this stretches the rotator cuff, which stabilizes the arm as you swing.

2. Trunk Forward Flexion: From a standing position, bend forward and grasp your ankles, bending your knees as necessary. Now straighten until you achieve a comfortable stretch. Loosening the lower body increases the range of motion of your swing.

3. Shoulder Blade Spread: To stretch the muscles that control the shoulder blades, grab your left elbow with your right hand and turn left shoulder under chin. Use left hand to grab right elbow and turn right shoulder under chin.

4. Crunch: The best way to golf proof the lower back is to strengthen the abs. With one hand behind your head in a sit up position, move your elbow toward the opposite knee, raising your shoulders six to eight inches off the ground. Do two sets of ten to fifteen reps. Switch hands and alternate.

5. The Empty Can: Another good rotator cuff exercise. Holding light weights at your sides, with your thumbs pointed down, slowly raise your arms forward until they

are at thirty-degree angle to your body. Keeping your elbows slightly flexed lift your arms out and up, almost to shoulder level.

6. Wrist-Up Curls: Stronger forearms wrists and hand will help steady your grip for the short game and add power of the tee. Sit on a chair with a dumbbell in your right hand and rest your right forearm on your right thigh, with your hand extended beyond the knee and the palm facing upwards. Slowly raise and lower the dumbbell without lifting your arm. Repeat with the other arm.

7. Wrist-Down Curls Technique and benefits are the same as for wrist-up curls, but with your palm facing downward.

Sources

"Golf and sex . . ."
Hobbs, Michael (1972*) The Golf Quotation Book*
Barnes & Noble Inc.: New York

"The main idea in golf . . ."
Jones, Robert "Bobby" Tyre (1966) *Golf Is My Game*
Doubleday & Company: New York

"There's a school . . ."
Jones, Robert "Bobby" Tyre (1966) *Golf Is My Game*
Doubleday & Company: New York

In the end Palmer's major championships. . .
Arnold Palmer and James Dodson (1999) *A Golfer's Life*
Ballentine Books: New York

"I played . . ."
Montville, Leigh (2006)
The Life and Times of Babe Ruth
Broadway Books, New York

Babe Ruth
Jane Levy (2018) *The Big Fella*
Harper Collins Publishers
New York

Alex Morrison
Interview with Grantland Rice
www.curedmygolfslice.com

Ben Hogan

"No teacher . . ."
"Early in his . . ."
"In the 1930's . . ."
"Bill Melhorn. . ."
Dodson, James (2004) *Ben Hogan: An American Life*
Doubleday: New York, London, Toronto, Sydney, Auckland

"Hennie Bogan . . ."
ESPN Interview 1991

"Bennie and Byron . . ."
"Asked some years . . ."
"I was mostly . . ."
"Watching. . ."
Dodson, James (2004) *Ben Hogan: An American Life*
Doubleday: New York, London, Toronto, Sydney, Auckland

"There's no doubt . . ."
"If you ever heard . . ."
Dodson, James (2004*) Ben Hogan: An American Life*
Doubleday: New York, London, Toronto, Sydney, Auckland

I.B. Nobody's Philosophy's

"You must learn . . ."
"You must not . . ."
"What we use . . ."
"The hands and . . ."
Boomer, Percy (1946*) On Learning Golf*
Alfred A. Knopf: New York

"What do the hands do?"
Hogan, Ben with Herbert Warren Wind / Drawings by Anthony Ravielli (1957)

Ben Hogan's Five Lessons: The Modern Fundamentals of Golf
A.S. Barnes & Company: New York

"My belief . . ."
Jones, Robert "Bobby" Trye Jr. (1959) *Golf Is My Game*
Doubleday & Company, Inc.: New York

"The three basic feels . . ."
Boomer, Percy (1946) *On Learning Golf*
Alfred A. Knopf: New York

Setup

"It is essential . . ."
Jones, Robert "Bobby" Tyre (1959) *Golf Is My Game*
Doubleday & Company:- New York

"The difference . . ."
"The only way . . ."
Boomer, Percy (1946) *On Learning Golf*
Alfred A. Knopf: New York

"I feel that . . ."
"I never . . ."
Nicklaus, Jack with Ken Bowden Illustrations by Jim McQueen
(1974)
Golf My Way
Simon & Schuster: New York

Grip

Picture Vardon Grip
Snead, Sam (1975) with Larry Sheehan/Technical Editor Ken
Bowden/Illustrations by Jim McQueen
Sam Snead Teaches You His Simple "Key" Approach to Golf
Atheneum: New York

Picture Interlocking Grip
Nicklaus, Jack with Ken Bowden Illustrations by Jim McQueen
(1974)
Golf My Way
Simon & Schuster: New York

"In a good grip. . ."
"With the back . . ."
"Crook the forefinger. . ."
"Now just close. . ."
Illustration - left hand
Hogan, Ben with Herbert Warren Wind / Drawings by Anthony
Ravielli (1957)
Ben Hogan's Five Lessons: The Modern Fundamentals of Golf
A. S. Barnes & Company: New York

"The right hand . . ."
Snead, Sam (1975) with Larry Sheehan/Technical Editor Ken
Bowden/Illustrations by Jim McQueen
Sam Snead Teaches You His Simple "Key" Approach to Golf
Atheneum: New York

"The muscles . . ."
Illustrations – right hand
"A word further. . ."
Hogan, Ben with Herbert Warren Wind / Drawings by Anthony
Ravielli (1957)
Ben Hogan's Five Lessons: The Modern Fundamentals of Golf
A. S. Barnes & Company: New York

Illustration – Vardon Grip
Snead, Sam (1975) with Larry Sheehan/Technical Editor Ken
Bowden/Illustrations by Jim McQueen
Sam Snead Teaches You His Simple "Key" Approach to Golf
Atheneum: New York

"The pressure . . ."
Hagen, Walter and Margaret Seaton Heck. (1956)
The Walter Hagen Story by the Haig Himself
Simon and Schuster

"The only way I know . . .
Jones, Robert "Bobby" Tyre (1959) *Golf Is My Game*
Doubleday & Company: New York

"Whatever you do . . ."
"I don't ever . . .
Nelson, Byron with Larry Dennis (1976)
"Shape Your Swing the Modern Way"
Golf Digest, Inc.: Connecticut

"In a way . . ."
Snead, Sam (1975) with Larry Sheehan/Technical Editor Ken
Bowden/Illustrations by Jim McQueen
Sam Snead Teaches You His Simple "Key" Approach to Golf
Atheneum: New York

"He showed . . ."
Arnold Palmer and James Dodson (1999) *A Golfer's Life*
Ballantine Books: New York

"The standard grip is the . . ."
Hogan, Ben with Herbert Warren Wind / Drawings by Anthony
Ravielli (1957)
Ben Hogan's Five Lessons: The Modern Fundamentals of Golf
A. S. Barnes & Company: New York

Arms – Setting up the Triangle

"Keeping the arms . . ."
Hagen, Walter and Margaret Seaton Heck.
The Walter Hagen Story by the Haig Himself
Simon and Schuster, 1956

"Ben Hogan . . ."
Snead, Sam with Al Stump (1962) *The Education of a Golfer*
Simon and Schuster: New York

"The arms . . ."
"Most . . ."
"It is . . ."
Boomer, Percy (1946) *On Learning Golf*
Alfred A. Knopf: New York

"Keep your left arm . . ."
Golf Range & Recreation Report March/April 1995

Personal interview

"A word of emphasis . . ."
"As your arms . . ."
Illustration
Hogan, Ben with Herbert Warren Wind / Drawings by Anthony
Ravielli (1957)
Ben Hogan's Five Lessons: The Modern Fundamentals of Golf
A. S. Barnes & Company: New York

Lower Body: Stance, Posture, Ball Position

"The value of perfect . . ."
Hagen, Walter and Margaret Seaton Heck.
The Walter Hagen Story by the Haig Himself
Simon and Schuster, 1956

"Never . . ."
Nelson, Byron (1946) *Winning Golf*
A.S. Barnes & Company: New York

"Many a golfer . . ."
"The feet should . . ."
"You should bend your. . ."

Hogan, Ben with Herbert Warren Wind / Drawings by Anthony
Ravielli (1957)
Ben Hogan's Five Lessons: The Modern Fundamentals of Golf
A. S. Barnes & Company: New York

"You know why. . ."
Dodson, James (2004*) Ben Hogan: An American Life*
Doubleday: New York, London, Toronto, Sydney, Auckland

Stance, Posture

Illustrations/Drawing
Hogan, Ben with Herbert Warren Wind / Drawings by Anthony
Ravielli (1957)
Ben Hogan's Five Lessons: The Modern Fundamentals of Golf
A. S. Barnes & Company - New York

Ball Position

"The basic objective. . ."
Nicklaus, Jack with Ken Bowden Illustrations by Jim McQueen
(1974)
Golf My Way
Simon & Schuster: New York

Alignment

"I would find a . . ."
"Whatever alignment . . ."
"You will instinctively . . ."
Nicklaus, Jack with Ken Bowden Illustrations by Jim McQueen
(1974)
Golf My Way
Simon & Schuster: New York

Waggling

"Waggle spontaneously . . ."
Hagen, Walter and Margaret Seaton Heck.
The Walter Hagen Story by the Haig Himself
Simon and Schuster, 1956

"At the moment . . ."
"The essence . . .
Nelson, Byron (1946) *Winning Golf*
A.S. Barnes & Company: New York

"Then the waggle . . ."
"Unless you feel . . ."
Boomer, Percy (1946) *On Learning Golf*
Alfred A. Knopf: New York

"The main thing . . ."
Nelson, Byron with Larry Dennis (1976)
Shape Your Swing the Modern Way
Simon & Schuster: New York

"If you do waggle . . ."
Nicklaus, Jack with Ken Bowden Illustrations by Jim McQueen
(1974) *Golf My Way*
Simon & Schuster: New York

"Hogan, wrote Cary Middlecoff . . ."
The Fundamentals of Hogan, David Ledbetter
(2000) Sleeping Bear Press Chelsea, MI
Doubleday A Division of Random House New York, NY

"The bridge . . ."
"The rhythm. . ."
Hogan, Ben with Herbert Warren Wind / Drawings by Anthony
Ravielli (1957)

Ben Hogan's Five Lessons: The Modern Fundamentals of Golf
A.S. Barnes & Company - New York

Photo of Ben Hogan
The Fundamentals of Hogan David Ledbetter
(2000) Sleeping Bear Press Chelsea, MI
Doubleday, a Division of Random House New York, NY

Illustration
Hogan, Ben with Herbert Warren Wind / Drawings by Anthony
Ravielli (1957)
Ben Hogan's Five Lessons: The Modern Fundamentals of Golf
A.S. Barnes & Company - New York

Takeaway
"There is no . . ."
"The triangle. . ."
"The wrists cock . . ."
Boomer, Percy (1946) *On Learning Golf*
Alfred A. Knopf: New York

"At no time . . ."
Nelson, Byron (1946) *Winning Golf*
A. S. Barnes & Company: New York

"When you swing back . . ."
Penick, Harvey with Bud Shrake (1992)
*Harvey Penick's Little Red Book Lessons and Teachings from a Lifetime
in Golf*
Simon & Schuster: New York

"The wrist cock . . ."
Snead, Sam with Al Stump (1962) *The Education of a Golfer*
Simon & Schuster: New York

"I believe you . . ."
Nicklaus, Jack with Ken Bowden Illustrations by Jim McQueen

(1974) *Golf My Way*
Simon & Schuster: New York

"I once heard. . ."
Nelson, Byron with Larry Dennis (1976)
"Shape Your Swing the Modern Way"
Golf Digest, Inc.: Connecticut

"The clubhead . . ."
"The two danger . . ."
"The initial movement. . ."
Jones, Robert "Bobby" Tyre (1966) *Bobby Jones on Golf*
Doubleday & Company: New York

"I just try . . ."
"When I'm trying . . ."
"Footwork, balance . . ."
"If your feet . . ."
Snead, Sam (1975)
with Larry Sheehan/Technical Editor Ken Bowden/Illustrations by
Jim McQueen
Sam Snead Teaches You His Simple "Key" Approach to Golf
Atheneum: New York

"Then from about . . ."
Snead, Sam with Al Stump (1962) *The Education of a Golfer*
Simon & Schuster: New York

"If he executes . . ."
Hogan, Ben with Herbert Warren Wind / Drawings by Anthony
Ravielli (1957)
Ben Hogan's Five Lessons: The Modern Fundamentals of Golf
A.S. Barnes & Company: New York

"To accomplish . . ."
Tony Lema with Bud Harvey (1966) *Champagne Tony's Golf Tips*
McGraw-Hill Book Company: New York

Illustration
Designed and Produced by Greenstone Roberts Advertising/Florida
(1990)
PGA Teaching Manual: The Art and Science of Golf Instruction
PGA of America: Florida

Staying on Plane throughout the Backswing

"Timing and hesitation . . .
Hagen, Walter and Margaret Seaton Heck.
The Walter Hagen Story by the Haig Himself
Simon and Schuster, 1956

"When your forward shoulder . . ."
Golf Digest article

Personal interview

"Visualize the backswing . . ."
"The center. . ."
Hogan, Ben with Herbert Warren Wind / Drawings by Anthony
Ravielli (1957)
Ben Hogan's Five Lessons: The Modern Fundamentals of Golf
A.S. Barnes & Company: New York

Pictures
Designed and Produced by Greenstone Roberts Advertising/Florida
(1990)
PGA Teaching Manual: The Art and Science of Golf Instruction
PGA of America: Florida

Illustration
Hogan, Ben with Herbert Warren Wind / Drawings by Anthony
Ravielli (1957)
Ben Hogan's Five Lessons: The Modern Fundamentals of Golf
A. S. Barnes & Company: New York

Initiating the Downswing

"The trunk muscles . . ."
"The only one . . ."
Jones, Robert "Bobby" Tyre (1966) *Bobby Jones on Golf*
Doubleday & Company: New York

"It is . . ."
Jones, Robert Trye (Bobby) Jr. (1959) *Golf Is My Game*
Doubleday & Company, Inc.: New York

"As the down swing . . ."
"I should say . . ."
"No matter . . ."
Jones, Robert "Bobby" Tyre (1966) *Bobby Jones on Golf*
Doubleday & Company: New York

"And we will . . ."
"So we must . . ."
"The clutch . . ."
"The power is . . ."
Boomer, Percy (1946) *On Learning Golf*
Alfred A. Knopf: New York

"The left hip . . ."
"It slowed me . . ."
Snead, Sam with Al Stump (1962) *The Education of a Golfer*
Simon & Schuster: New York

"It is important . . ."
"Feeling leisurely . . ."
Nelson, Byron (1946) *Winning Golf*
A. S. Barnes & Company: New York

"The hips initiate . . ."
Hogan, Ben with Herbert Warren Wind / Drawings by Anthony
Ravielli (1957)
Ben Hogan's Five Lessons: The Modern Fundamentals of Golf
A.S. Barnes & Company: New York

"If you clear the left hip early . . ."
Dodson, James (2004) *Ben Hogan: An American Life*
Doubleday: New York, London, Toronto, Sydney, Auckland

"To start the . . ."
Golf magazine article

"You start the downswing . . ."
Nicklaus, Jack with Ken Bowden Illustrations by Jim McQueen
(1974) *Golf My Way*
Simon & Schuster: New York

Picture
The Fundamentals of Hogan
David Ledbetter
(2000) Sleeping Bear Press Chelsea, MI
Doubleday, a Division of Random House New York, NY

Picture
PGA Teaching Manual: The Art and Science of Golf Instruction
PGA of America: Florida
Designed and Produced by Greenstone Roberts Advertising/Florida
(1990)

Picture
The Fundamentals of Hogan
David Ledbetter
(2000) Sleeping Bear Press Chelsea, MI
Doubleday, a Division of Random House New York, NY

Hitting Through in One Cohesive Movement

"The ordinary golfer . . ."
"Because it is no use . . ."
"Timing then . . ."
"Golf rhythm
"As I . . ."
Boomer, Percy (1946) *On Learning Golf*
Alfred A. Knopf: New York

"Always remember . . ."
Nelson, Byron (1946) *Winning Golf*
A. S. Barnes & Company: New York

"The difference . . ."
Snead, Sam with Al Stump (1962) *The Education of a Golfer*
Simon & Schuster: New York

"Your problem . . .
Nelson, Byron with Larry Dennis (1976)
Shape Your Swing the Modern Way
Simon & Schuster: New York

"The movement . . ."
Hogan, Ben with Herbert Warren Wind / Drawings by Anthony
Ravielli (1957)
Ben Hogan's Five Lessons: The Modern Fundamentals of Golf
A. S. Barnes & Company: New York

Impact

Illustrations
Nicklaus, Jack with Ken Bowden Illustrations by Jim McQueen
(1974) *Golf My Way*
Simon & Schuster: New York

Picture – Sports Illustrated

"By crucial strokes
"Above all . . ."
Jones, Robert "Bobby" Tyre (1959) *Golf Is My Game*
Doubleday & Company: New York

"One important factor . . ."
Nelson, Byron (1946) Winning Golf
A. S. Barnes & Company: New York

"The ultimate judge. . ."
Hogan, Ben with Herbert Warren Wind / Drawings by Anthony Ravielli (1957)
Ben Hogan's Five Lessons: The Modern Fundamentals of Golf
A. S. Barnes & Company: New York

"I let the results . . ."
Snead, Sam with Al Stump (1962) *The Education of a Golfer*
Simon & Schuster: New York

"Yes. . ."
Johnnie Miller article

"A perfectly straight . . ."
Hobbs, Michael (1972) *The Golf Quotation Book*
Barnes & Noble Inc.: New York

Illustration
Designed and Produced by Greenstone Roberts Advertising/Florida (1990)
PGA Teaching Manual: The Art and Science of Golf Instruction
PGA of America: Florida

Illustrations – Figure 1 through Figure 10
Jones, Robert "Bobby" Trye Jr. (1959) *Golf Is My Game*
Doubleday & Company Inc.: New York

The Short Game

"Three of these . . ."
Hagen, Walter and Margaret Seaton Heck
The Walter Hagen Story by the Haig Himself
Simon & Schuster, 1956

"The secret of golf . . ."
Golf Digest article

"I want you to feel . . ."
"The short shot . . ."
Boomer, Percy (1946) *On Learning Golf*
Alfred A. Knopf: New York

"The two most important rules . . ."
Jones, Robert "Bobby" Tyre (1966) *Bobby Jones on Golf*
Doubleday & Company: New York

"In other words . . ."
Jones, Robert "Bobby" Tyre (1959) *Golf Is My Game*
Doubleday & Company: New York

"On pitching . . ."
Jones, Robert "Bobby" Tyre (1966) *Bobby Jones on Golf*
Doubleday & Company: New York

"Most good golfers . . ."
Jones, Robert "Bobby" Tyre (1959) *Golf Is My Game*
Doubleday & Company: New York

"It is demonstrably . . ."
"One should avoid . . ."
Jones, Robert "Bobby" Tyre (1966) *Bobby Jones on Golf*
Doubleday & Company: New York

"The turning of the body . . ."
Jones, Robert "Bobby" Tyre (1959) *Golf Is My Game*
Doubleday & Company: New York

"Many golfers . . ."
"In studying the finish. . ."
Nelson, Byron (1946) *Winning Golf*
A. S. Barnes & Company: New York

"Jones complimented . . ."
"To be able to scramble. . ."
Snead, Sam with Al Stump (1962) *The Education of a Golfer*
Simon & Schuster: New York

"To be able to scramble . . ."
Snead, Sam with Al Stump (1962) *The Education of a Golfer*
Simon & Schuster: New York

"Try to play . . ."
Personal interview

"Hogan's Last Competitive Round"
"The commonly held view . . ."
Dodson, James (2004) *Ben Hogan: An American Life*
Doubleday: New York, London, Toronto, Sydney, Auckland

Pictures – Fred Couples
Golf Digest article

Routines

"You don't try to change. . .
Golf Digest article

"Our first passage . . ."
Murphy, Michael (1972) *Golf in the Kingdom*
Dell Publishing Co. Inc.: New York

"But when I play . . ."
Boomer, Percy (1946) *On Learning Golf*
Alfred A. Knopf: New York

Hogan's Routine
Sampson, Kurt (1996) *Hogan*
Broadway Books: New York

"He had a unvarying routine. . ."
Golf Digest article

Payne Stewart recorded conversation . . .
Monterey County Herald
June 15–18, 1999

Putting Concepts

"There is nothing . . ."
Jones, Robert "Bobby" Tyre(1966) *Bobby Jones on Golf*
Doubleday & Co.: New York

Jack Nicklaus
Personal observation

"The putting stroke . . .
"My two . . ."
George Low with Al Barkow (1983)
The Master of Putting: Classic Secrets of a Putting Legend
Atheneum: New York

"The secret . . ."
Hagen, Walter and Margaret Seaton Heck.
The Walter Hagen Story by the Haig Himself
Simon & Schuster, 1956

"I cannot overstress . . ."
"Once I have made. . ."
"After determining. . ."
Golf Digest article

"Even on the smoothest . . ."
Golf Digest article

"Look for a . . ."
Personal interview

"I have holed . . ."
Jones, Robert "Bobby" Trye Jr. (1966) *Bobby Jones on Golf*
Doubleday & Company Inc.: New York

"Hold the putter . . ."
George Low with Al Barkow (1983)
The Master of Putting: Classic Secrets of a Putting Legend
Atheneum: New York

"Rest the putter . . ."
Personal Interview

"Light but aggressive . . ."
Personal interview

"Hold the club . . ."
Personal interview

"To avoid movement . . ."
"Your eyes . . ."
"If you expect . . ."
"Take a practice . . ."
George Low with Al Barkow (1983)
The Master of Putting: Classic Secrets of a Putting Legend
Atheneum: New York

"Bobby Locke . . ."
"The most helpful. . ."
"I have always. . ."
Golf Digest article

"I'm think of the pen. . ."
Golf Digest article

"After the rehearsal . . ."
George Low with Al Barkow (1983)
The Master of Putting: Classic Secrets of a Putting Legend
Atheneum: New York

"Continuous smooth movement . . ."
Golf Digest article

"All I can do . . ."
Dodson, James (2004) *Ben Hogan: An American Life*
Doubleday: New York, London, Toronto, Sydney, Auckland

"Still hog . . ."
Personal interview

"After Arnold Palmer . . ."
George Low with Al Barkow (1983)
The Master of Putting: Classic Secrets of a Putting Legend
Atheneum: New York

"Staying calm . . ."
Lema, Tony with Gwilyn S. Brown (1964)
Golfers' Gold: An Inside View of the Pro Tour
Little, Brown & Company: Boston, Toronto

"If you become responsive . . ."
Gallwey, W. Timothy (1974) *The Inner Game of Tennis*
Random House, NY

"Walter Travis . . . "
Jones, Robert "Bobby" Trye Jr. (1966) *Bobby Jones on Golf*
Doubleday & Company Inc.: New York

"The picture I want uppermost in my mind is of the line . . ."
Jones, Robert "Bobby" Trye. (1959) *Golf Is My Game*
Doubleday & Company Inc.: New York

"As Jimmy Demaret. . .
Dodson, James (2004) *Ben Hogan: An American Life*
Doubleday: New York, London, Toronto, Sydney, Auckland

"I've still got the hole . . ."
Golf Digest article

Centering

"As with the golf swing. . ."
"The power is . . ."
Boomer, Percy (1946) *On Learning Golf*
Alfred A. Knopf: New York

"whenever in breath . . ."
"Consider . . ."
"Place your whole . . ."
"Bathe in the sound . . ."
"Imagine . . ."
"Feel your . . ."
"When . . ."
"Abide in some . . ."
"At the point . . ."
"Without support . . ."
"With mouth slightly open . . ."
"Simply by looking . . ."
Reps, Paul (1957)
Zen Bones, Zen Flesh: A Collection of Zen and PreZen Writings
Charles E. Tuttle Co.: Rutland, Vermont, Tokyo, Japan

Moving from center

"I like to feel . . ."
Golf Digest article

Stroke happens-swing & impact

"If you concentrate . . .
Snead, Sam (1975)
with Larry Sheehan/Technical Editor Ken Bowden/Illustrations by
Jim McQueen
Sam Snead Teaches You His Simple "Key" Approach to Golf

"The key feature . . ."
George Low with Al Barkow (1983)
The Master of Putting: Classic Secrets of a Putting Legend
Atheneum: New York

Ted Neist
Personal Interview

Graeme Courts
Sports Illustrated article

"Shit, man, . . ."
Personal interview

"Hagen had the . . ."
Snead, Sam with Al Stump (1962) The Education of a Golfer
Simon & Schuster: New York

"Look at the ball . . ."
"Judge 'em by sound . . ."
Golf Digest

"I don't putt . . ."
Dodson, James (2004) *Ben Hogan: An American Life*
Doubleday: New York, London, Toronto, Sydney, Auckland

These hold to be true about putting. . .

"Until all . . ."
Boomer, Percy (1946) *On Learning Golf*
Alfred A. Knopf: New York

"Firm hitting . . ."
Jones, Robert "Bobby" Tyre (1966) *Bobby Jones on Golf*
Doubleday & Co.: New York

"The actual. . ."
Golf Digest article

"On some holes . . ."
Hagen, Walter and Margaret Seaton Heck (1956)
The Walter Hagen Story by the Haig Himself
Simon & Schuster: New York

"I could make . ."
"As I saw it. . ."
"Confidence. . "
Snead, Sam with Al Stump (1962) *The Education of a Golfer*
Simon & Schuster: New York

"One has to be . . ."
Lema, Tony with Gwilyn S. Brown (1964)
Golfers' Gold: An Inside View of the Pro Tour
Little, Brown & Company: Boston, Toronto

Pictures:
Golf Digest, Walter Hagen
Golf Digest, Bobby Locke
Golf Digest, Jerry Barber

Locke's Seven Steps
Golf Digest article

Picture
Golf Digest,- Jack Nicklaus

Mental Aspects

"Competitive golf . . ."
Jones, Robert "Bobby" Trye Jr. (1959) *Golf Is My Game*
Doubleday & Company Inc.: New York

"Hogan hit the shot . . ."
Personal Interview

"The good golfer
Boomer, Percy (1946) *On Learning Golf*
Alfred A. Knopf: New York

"The same man . . ."
"His ability . . ."
Dodson, James (2004) *Ben Hogan: An American Life*
Doubleday: New York, London, Toronto, Sydney, Auckland

"The practice swings . . ."
Snead, Sam with Al Stump (1962) *The Education of a Golfer*
Simon & Schuster: New York

"When I swing . . ."
"I limit myself . . ."
"I don't go into a . . ."
Snead, Sam (1975)
with Larry Sheehan/Technical Editor Ken Bowden/Illustrations by
Jim McQueen
Sam Snead Teaches You His Simple "Key" Approach to Golf
Atheneum: New York

"Look for a lighthouse . . ."
Personal interview

"Pictures, feelings, abstracts . . ."
"Forget about . . ."
"How does Picasso paint . . ."
"Learn to program . . ."
Personal interview

"He told me . . ."
Golf World article

"Learning to see . . ."
"You have to . . ."
"Visualize . . ."
"We have to let. . ."
"The mind. . ."
Gallwey, Timothy W (1974) *The Inner Game of Tennis*
Random House: New York

"Close yer eyes . . ."
"Remember the . . ."
"Put a symbol . . ."
Murphy, Michael (1972) *Golf in the Kingdom*
Dell Publishing Company: New York

"You can't think and hit at the same time . . ."
Berra, (1998)
Yogi *The Yogi Book*
Workman Publishing: New York

When the left brain interferes

"No matter how . . ."
Jones, Robert "Bobby" Trye Jr. (1959) *Golf Is My Game*
Doubleday & Company Inc.: New York

"Guldahl . . ."
Dodson, James (2004) *Ben Hogan: An American Life*
Doubleday: New York London Toronto Sydney Auckland

"Pap would tell me . . ."
Arnold Palmer and James Dodson
A Golfer's Life
Ballantine Books: New York (1999)

Playing by Feel

"In order to play well . . ."
"By training himself . . ."
Jones, Robert "Bobby" Tyre (1966) *Bobby Jones on Golf*
Doubleday & Company: New York

"Walter Hagen . . ."
"Control through remembered . . ."
"But when . . ."
"Knowledge and thought . . ."
"As I've said . . ."
"These movements . . ."
"When you think . . ."
Boomer, Percy (1946) *On Learning Golf*
Alfred A. Knopf: New York

"The game. . ."
Dodson, James (2004) *Ben Hogan: An American Life*
Doubleday: New York London Toronto Sydney Auckland

"Once your mechanics. . ."
Personal interview

Concentration

"So when a . . ."
"When you think . . ."
Boomer, Percy (1946) *On Learning Golf*
Alfred A. Knopf: New York

"In my mind today . . ."
Jones, Robert "Bobby" Trye Jr. (1959) *Golf Is My Game*
Doubleday & Company Inc.: New York

"The expert . . ."
Jones, Robert Bobby" Trye Jr. (1966) *Bobby Jones on Golf*
Doubleday & Co.: New York

"To remind yourself . . ."
Snead, Sam (1975)
with Larry Sheehan/technical editor Ken Bowden/Illustrations by
Jim McQueen
Sam Snead Teaches You His Simple "Key" Approach to Golf
Atheneum: New York

"Runyan knows how to finish . . ."
Dodson, James (2004) *Ben Hogan: An American Life*
Doubleday: New York, London, Toronto, Sydney, Auckland

"When I swing . . ."
Snead, Sam (1975)
with Larry Sheehan/Technical Editor Ken Bowden/Illustrations by
Jim McQueen
Sam Snead Teaches You His Simple "Key" Approach to Golf
Atheneum: New York

"The golf swing . . ."
Snead, Sam (1975)
with Larry Sheehan/technical editor Ken Bowden/Illustrations by
Jim McQueen
Sam Snead Teaches You His Simple "Key" Approach to Golf
Atheneum: New York

"If you don't . . ."
Earl Woods (1998)
Training a Tiger: A Father's Guide to Raising a Winner in Golf & Life
Harper Collins: New York

"This profound notion. . ."
Dodson, James (2004) *Ben Hogan: An American Life*
Doubleday: New York London Toronto Sydney Auckland

Psycho-Cybernetics: A New Way to Get More Living Out of Life
Maxwell Maltz 1960, Prentice Hall, Inc.
Englewood Cliffs, New Jersey

"Just imagine . . ."
Sports Illustrated article

Stedman Graham
Personal experience

John Brodie
Golf Digest Article

Temperament

"If you wish to hide . . ."
"I suppose . . ."
Boomer, Percy (1946) *On Learning Golf*
Alfred A. Knopf: New York

"Is there a psychology . . ."
Nelson, Byron (1946) *Winning Golf*
A. S. Barnes & Company: New York

"An old timer . . ."
"The lesson . . ."
Snead, Sam with Al Stump (1962) *The Education of a Golfer*
Simon & Schuster: New York

"The right idea of course . . ."
"A great many . . ."
"Playing golf . . ."
The most important . . ."
Lema, Tony with Gwilyn S. Brown (1964)
Golfers' Gold: An Inside View of the Pro Tour
Little, Brown & Company: Boston, Toronto

"I never pray . . ."
Golf Digest

"Never break . . ."
"If you are . . ."
Golf: The Lore of the Links
1992 by Armand Eisen

"After losing. . ."
Golf World article

"Baseball is 90 percent . . ."
Berra, Yogi (1998)
The Yogi Book
Workman Publishing, New York

Tom Morris
Gotham Books - Penguin Group, NY 2008
Kevin Cook *Tommy's Honor*

Walter Hagen
Hagen, Walter and Margaret Seaton Heck.
The Walter Hagen Story by the Haig Himself
Simon & Schuster, 1956

Pictures of the Greats
Walter Hagen
Bobby Jones
Gene Sarazen
Ben Hogan
Byron Nelson
Sam Snead
Jack Nicklaus
Designed and Produced by Greenstone Roberts Advertising/Florida
(1990)
PGA Teaching Manual: The Art and Science of Golf Instruction
PGA of America: Florida

Northern California – circa 1966

Quiet Glory of a Driving Range Pro
Lucious Bateman
Spander, Art (1972) "Quiet Glory of a Driving Range Pro"
Golf Magazine, March 1972 Volume 14 No. 3

"Kids"
Contra Costa Times, July 12, 2009

Photos of the Greats
Arnold Palmer
Billy Casper
Lee Trevino
Designed and Produced by Greenstone Roberts Advertising/Florida
(1990)
PGA Teaching Manual: The Art and Science of Golf Instruction
PGA of America: Florida

"What we all . . ."
Snead, Sam with Al Stump (1962) *The Education of a Golfer*
Simon & Schuster: New York

Personal Interview
Ben Doyle
Kelly, Homer *The Golfing Machine*

"Inverse functioning. . ."
"Consider the pivot. . "
"Now it is really. . ."
Boomer, Percy (1946) *On Learning Golf*
Alfred A. Knopf: New York

At the Range

"The golf course . . ."
Jones, Robert "Bobby" Trye Jr. (1959) *Golf Is My Game*
Doubleday & Company Inc.: New York
"Before Ben . . ."
Dodson, James (2004) *Ben Hogan: An American Life*
Doubleday: New York, London, Toronto, Sydney, Auckland

"It was inconceivable . . ."
Arnold Palmer and James Dodson
Ballantine Books New York (1999) *A Golfer's Life*

Index

About the Author

I. B. Nobody, a Northern California native, was taught to play by Lucious Bateman—a golf instructor whose insights assisted seven players who played the tour from 1950s to the 1970s. After his death in 1972, the author went about sourcing the best players in the Northern California region for instruction. Reading and highlighting quotes from the masters' books—Bobby Jones, Walter Hagen, Ben Hogan, Sam Snead, Byron Nelson, Jack Nicklaus, Arnold Palmer—and the meticulous notes from those lessons and real-life experiences from his days caddying are interwoven in a concise, simple process to understanding the game of golf.